FANTASTIC
Frankie
and the BRAIN-DRAIN Machine

Mr Blewitt

Mrs Blewitt

Dr Gore

Alphonsine

Frankie Blewitt

For
my brilliant friend Daisy
and
the fantastic Thomas

First published in Great Britain in 2011 by Simon and Schuster UK Ltd, a CBS company.
Simon & Schuster UK Ltd
1st Floor, 222 Gray's Inn Road, London WC1X 8HB

www.simonandschuster.co.uk

Text copyright © Anna Kemp 2011
Illustrations copyright © Alex T. Smith 2011

The right of Anna Kemp and Alex T. Smith to be identified as the author and illustrator
of this work respectively has been asserted by them in accordance with sections 77 and
78 of the Copyright, Designs and Patents Act, 1988.

A CIP catalogue record for this book is available from the British Library.

ISBN 978-1-84738-936-7

1 3 5 7 9 10 8 6 4 2

Printed in the UK by CPI Cox and Wyman Ltd, Reading, Berkshire RG1 8EX

ANNA KEMP

FANTASTIC Frankie
AND THE BRAIN-DRAIN MACHINE

Illustrated by
Alex T Smith

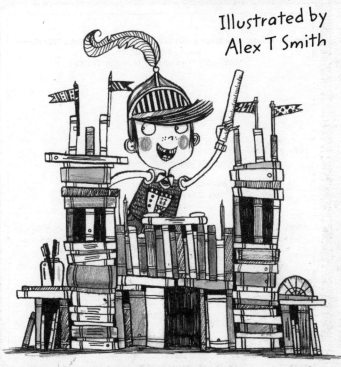

SIMON AND SCHUSTER

CHAPTER ONE
A-Bit-Of-a-Dreamer

Some kids win all the prizes. You know who they are. The ones who are always top of the class, or first over the finishing line, or lifting that massive shiny trophy on sports day. The ones who are always picked to go on the cover of the school magazine, or to shake the mayor's hand, or to look after the class hamster at the weekends – even though you looked after the hamster all week long and it didn't die or turn green or anything! Well, Peggy Parfitt was one of those kids. If there was a prize to be won she just went out there and won it: science prizes, art prizes, looking-after-the-hamster-prizes, not-picking-your-nose-prizes. OK, I made that last one up. But if there had been a prize for not picking your nose, Peggy would have won it hands down, along with the not-staring-out-of–the-window-prize and the not-putting-a-frog-in-teacher's-pocket-prize and... you get the idea.

Everyone loved Peggy. The teachers fought to have her in their class, her parents were as proud as parrots, even the hamster liked Peggy best – which was *really* unfair. Peggy was everybody's hero. But, unfortunately Peggy went to the zoo one day and got eaten by a tiger. So Peggy won't be the hero of our story. We will have to make do with that kid in the corner with the grubby knees. His name is Frankie Blewitt. Are you listening Frankie? Oh good. Now we can begin.

Frankie Blewitt would have done anything to

make his parents proud. But Mr and Mrs Blewitt were impossible to please. If he got a silver star for his school project, Mr Blewitt wouldn't pat him on the back and say well done. He would just shout, 'Silver? Cheap and nasty! Where's the gold!' Or, if he won the dressing-up race on sports day, Mrs Blewitt wouldn't ruffle his hair with pride. Instead she would say, 'Ugh, Frankie what are you wearing?! Get in the car now!' The truth is, Frankie Blewitt could have walked on water and his parents would have demanded to know why he couldn't tapdance on it as well. So when, one soggy December afternoon, Frankie Blewitt saw the postman delivering his school report he climbed into his wardrobe and shut the door.

As you can imagine, Frankie didn't look forward to his school report one little bit. However good he had been and however hard he had tried, it was never good enough for his mum and dad.

I'm not saying he was a dimwit – he wasn't. But Frankie wasn't very good at writing and counting and taking tests. When he looked at his schoolbooks, all the letters muddled together like alphabet soup, and he began to think about all the things he would rather be doing like flying helicopters or solving crimes or rescuing a dog from a burning building. 'If I was stuck on a desert island and had nothing to eat except sand,' Frankie would think to himself, 'I wouldn't need to know my seven times-table. I would need to know survival skills, like how to make a house out of coconuts. Why don't they teach that at school?' Then a voice far off in the distance would call, 'Frankie Blewitt!' the voice would get closer, 'Frankie Blewitt! What did I just say?' and Frankie would have to reply 'Sorry, Mrs Grimmet, I wasn't really listening'. School-report day was always bad news for Frankie Blewitt. But, as Frankie was soon to discover, that day in December would turn out to be the worst one ever.

Frankie held his breath as Mr Blewitt thudded to the door to inspect the mail. He closed his eyes, crossed his fingers and hoped that maybe this time would be different. Maybe he would get an 'A' or something and his parents would take him out for pizza and let him eat all the topping without the crust, or maybe...

'FRRRRRRRRANKIE!' The walls of the house shook, 'WHERE ARE YOU?' Frankie squeezed himself into the corner of the wardrobe as Mr Blewitt's footsteps thumped up the stairs. 'I KNOW YOU'RE IN HERE!' Mr Blewitt burst into the room and Frankie started to panic. He had seen a film about some children who escape through a magic wardrobe into a marvellous land and, in his fright, he pounded on the back panel, hoping it would open up and let him through. But all he got was some splinters in his knuckles and before he could say *Narnia*, the wardrobe doors swung wide open.

Mr Blewitt glared down at Frankie, snorting and flexing his shoulders like an enormous bull. Every muscle in Mr Blewitt's body was pumped up so tightly, Frankie thought that if he pricked his dad with a pin, he might shoot round the room like a balloon, then wrinkle up and drop to the floor. But he wasn't about to try it.

'You've got some EXPLAINING to do young man!' sneered Mr Blewitt. Then, pinching Frankie's left ear between his fingers, he dragged him down to the kitchen where Mrs Blewitt was sobbing extravagantly into a tea towel.

'My child is a delinquent, a no-hoper. And we gave him everything, EVERYTHING!' she howled like she was on TV or something.

'Just read what it says my precious peanut,' soothed Mr Blewitt. Mrs Blewitt wiped her smudgy eyes, and picked up Frankie's school report.

'Frankie,' sniffled Mrs Blewitt, 'has a marvellous imagination, but he is... a bit of a dreamer!'

'A-bit-of-a-dreamer,' repeated Mr Blewitt running his hand over the top of his head, which was completely flat as if he used it to bash down doors. 'Do you think I pay good money to those lousy teachers of yours...' He picked up the white booklet as if it were a snotty hanky, 'Do you think I spend my hard-earned cash, so that you can grow up to be A-BIT-OF-A-DREAMER? By the time I was your age,' he bellowed, 'I was captain of the rugby club, head-boy, prize-winner...'

'Milk monitor,' added Mrs Blewitt proudly.

'Milk monitor, AND I read the dictionary in

my lunch break! Do you think,' he went on, practically cooking with rage, 'that I could afford a spanking new house and a brand-new sports car and triple-quilted toilet paper if I spent my time floating off with the fairies like my nitwit son?'

'But, Dad,' Frankie protested, 'I try, it's just… it's hard.'

'Of course it's hard, when your head is stuffed full of that *marvellous imagination* of yours!' Mr Blewitt whipped out a red marker pen and drew a large "F" on the cover of Frankie's report. 'Can you read it?' Frankie nodded, 'Know what it stands for?' Frankie shook his head, 'Fail! "F" stands for Fail. It also stands for Frankie. There's only one way you're going to learn. No more toys, no more playtime, no more mucking about. You're eight years old. It's high time you thought about your future.'

Steaming like a kettle, Mr Blewitt rolled up

his sleeves, grabbed a bin bag and marched upstairs to Frankie's room. Any unlucky toy left lying around was immediately snatched up and thrown away – a pile of picture books, Frankie's sticker collection, his favourite toy castle. 'Time to focus!' bellowed Mr Blewitt, 'Time to get down to business!'

'Dad! Stop!' Frankie cried. But Mr Blewitt had made up his mind and there was absolutely no unmaking it. In went a robot, in went a jigsaw, in went a box of toy soldiers.

'This lot will make a nice little bonfire,' he hooted. Then, to Frankie's horror, he grabbed Albert, his beloved old teddy bear, and marched out the door.

'Albert! Albert!' Frankie yelled, but Mr Blewitt slammed the door behind him and turned the key.

Frankie ran to his bedroom window and

looked out into the garden. It was getting dark, but he could make out the hulking figure of Mr Blewitt stacking all of his things on to a heap of firewood. 'It's not fair! It's not fair!' he whispered as the flames whistled and roared. Frankie pressed his forehead against the glass and watched until his belongings had collapsed into a grey, smouldering heap. 'Albert!' he cried, and an angry tear spilled down his cheek.

Tat-Tat-Tat. There was a knock at the bedroom door. *Toc-Toc-Toc.* Frankie recognised the secret knock. A code known only to Frankie and one other very special person. The lock turned and the door was opened quickly and quietly. His old French nanny, Alphonsine, one finger pressed to her lips in silence, stepped into his room. She flicked her eyes from side to side to check she had not been followed then closed the door behind her.

'I found Monsieur Al-bear,' she whispered, producing the teddy bear from her apron pocket. Frankie sighed with relief.

'You're the greatest, Alphonsine,' he said, hugging her tightly, 'You're amazing!'

CHAPTER TWO
THE AMAZING ALPHONSINE

Alphonsine had lived with the Blewitts since Frankie was just a 'pea in ze pod.' She cooked, she cleaned, she polished Mr Blewitt's trophies, but most of all she looked after Frankie. Truth was, when Mrs Blewitt discovered she was pregnant, all she could think about was how lovely it would be to have a little girl that she could dress up like a dolly. So when the doctor told her she was expecting a boy, she felt downright cheated. The very next day she slapped an advert in the local paper for a nanny and housekeeper, and before long Alphonsine had parked her motorbike in the driveway and moved into the Blewitt's attic.

But Alphonsine was not your average nanny. Although she was over eighty years old, she was as strong as a tractor and as nimble as a bird. 'As long as I have my coffee in ze morning,' she would say as she took a chainsaw to an unruly tree, 'I can do anything!' And Frankie didn't dare doubt it. But Alphonsine always had an extra pair of hands (or rather paws) to help her out. Wherever Alphonsine went, Colette, her faithful French poodle, trotted swiftly behind. Now, you might think that French poodles are just yappy little fluffballs with no brains, but not Colette. Sure she was small and fluffy, but she was also completely fearless. When Attila, the neighbour's doberman, tried to steal a sausage from Alphonsine's shopping bag, Colette snapped and snarled so ferociously that Attila's owner couldn't get him to go back outside for a week. In fact, the only person more fearless than Alphonsine's poodle, was Alphonsine herself. She wasn't afraid of anyone – especially not Mr and Mrs Blewitt, and especially not when they burned Frankie's favourite things.

'Colette pull him out just in time!' whispered Alphonsine, dusting off Albert's singed fur and handing him to Frankie, 'A second later and Pouf! Goodbye Monsieur Al-bear.'

'Good girl, Colette!' said Frankie, ruffling the dog's curly white ears.

'Now you put on your pyjamas,' said Alphonsine, 'and I make us a chocolate hot.'

'A hot chocolate.' said Frankie absent-mindedly.

'Yes, yes,' Alphonsine tutted, 'zat is what I said!'

Alphonsine and Colette went up to the attic, leaving Frankie alone in his bedroom, which now felt emptier than ever. Only Albert and a few other lucky toys had survived Mr Blewitt's rampage. Everything that had been within grabbing-distance was gone – burnt to a crisp. Frankie sat on his bed and felt as empty as a shell. Maybe his father was right, maybe he *was* a no-hoper. I mean, what had he ever *achieved*. His classmates took home trophies and badges and their parents clapped them on prize-day. The only thing Frankie had ever taken home was headlice – and no one had thanked him for that. Frankie sighed, pulled on his pyjamas and sloped upstairs to Alphonsine's attic.

'Cheery up!' said Alphonsine, pulling up a half-broken rocking-chair, 'Life's not so bad!' She gave the saucepan a quick stir and the sweet smell of chocolate filled Frankie's nostrils. But it was going to take more than hot chocolate to lift Frankie's spirits today.

'I'll never be like my dad,' Frankie said. 'I'm a no-hoper.' Alphonsine narrowed her eyes and passed him his mug.

'Is zat what you want?' she said, 'You want to be like your dad?'

'Well I guess so.' said Frankie. 'I suppose…'

'Even though your dad is a big turnip?'

'No,' he said, 'I guess not. I don't want to be a turnip.'

'Well then!' cried Alphonsine, throwing her hands in the air, 'Ze REAL question is, what does FRANKIE want?' Frankie stared into his hot chocolate. He'd never asked himself that before. What did *he*, Frankie Blewitt, want? Alphonsine looked at him slyly, 'I bets I know.' she said. Then leaning towards him, she whispered, 'Frankie Blewitt wants ADVENTURE!' The word made the hairs on Frankie's head prickle.

'I don't know, Alfie,' he said, 'What do I know about adventure?'

'Ha!' cried Alphonsine, slapping her thigh, 'I tell you ALL about adventure!'

'Really?' said Frankie, staring at her in amazement.

'But of course! Just because I do not wear my knickers over my trousers like a super-action-hero, does not mean I have not had adventures. Drink your chocolate.' Frankie did as he was told. 'Now,' said Alphonsine, pulling her chair close to Frankie, 'look me in the eyes.' Frankie looked. 'Notice anything odd. Anything a little bit... bizarre?' Frankie looked hard. No, Alphonsine's eyes were their usual pebbly grey. 'Look closer,' said Alphonsine and, squinting suddenly, she popped out her left eye into the palm of her hand.

'AAAAAGHH!' Frankie screamed and spilt his drink all over his pyjamas.

'Don't worry my little cabbage. It is nothing,' said Alphonsine, tapping the eye with her nail. 'It is made of glass. I have had it always. When I was born, my grandfather opened the best bottle of

24

champagne, and PAF! The cork hit me straight in the eye. Too bad. There is worse things in life. You want to see?' Frankie slowly held out his hand. 'Now, me and my eye have had many, many adventures!'

'Really?' said Frankie, peering at it cautiously.

'But of course!' said Alphonsine, 'Look.' Alphonsine gripped the glass eyeball between her fingers, twisted it as if she were opening a jam jar, and *pop*, the eye split in two.

'During ze war,' Alphonsine explained, 'I was an agent for the French Resistance. We were fighting to free our country from the Nasty invaders. Sabotage was our job—'

'What's sabotage?' asked Frankie.

'Being a nuisance.' said Alphonsine. 'A spanner in the works. We would tamper with equipment, steal weapons, blow things up...'

'No way!'

'Yes way! I used this eye to transport tip-top-secret messages. I folded them up tiny tiny and popped them inside. It was very dangerous. Very important never to get caught. If the Nasties discovered you were working against them, then...' Alphonsine made a sound like tearing paper and drew her finger across her throat. Frankie shuddered. 'Ze Resistance was so tip-top-secret, agents sent coded messages to each other in the local newspaper.

'One day, I was waiting in my mother's shop, doing the crossword when I come across a clue: *What creature has eyes but cannot see?* Ha! Straight away I know this is a message for me.' Alphonsine tapped her glass eye and popped it back in the socket. 'I know that I have been selected for my first mission. I was so very proud.'

'What did you have to do?' asked Frankie, sitting up straight in his chair.

'It should have been as simple as an egg. I was to take a most important message to the barman at Café Cornichon in the next village. So I collect the message, pop it in my eye and set off on my bicycle. I cycle as fast as a weasel through the woods and through the fields and past patrols of enemy soldiers. When I get to Café Cornichon, I am as nervous as a lobster in a pot. I sit near the bar and I am waiting for the barman and I am munching the end of my baguette to calm my nerves, when what do I see but a Nasty officer having his lunch at the next table!'

'What did you do Alfie? What did you do?!' cried Frankie, rocking forward in his chair.

'Well, I choke on my baguette of course! And I am choking and choking and the waiter kindly wallops me on ze back. But he wallops me so hard, out pops my eye! I was horrified I tell you. So I am scrabbling about on the floor looking for my eye with the tip-top secret message in it, when I hear a shriek coming from the next table: "Vot is ZAT in my soup?!" And I look, and the officer is staring into his *soupe du jour*, white as a goat, and staring right back at him, is my eye! Well the officer feels quite sick of course so, lucky for me, he runs off to the toilets. I pluck the eye out of the soup, give it a quick wipe on my sleeve and slip it to the barman.' Alphonsine dusted her hands together as if she'd been kneading bread, 'Mission accomplished!'

'How many missions did you have?' asked Frankie.

'Oh, many many,' replied Alphonsine. 'It was necessary.'

'I wish somebody would give me a secret mission,' Frankie sighed.

'But you are a silly parrot!' laughed Alphonsine, slapping her knees, 'You don't wait for adventure. You MAKE adventure. You think astronauts just sit around and stare at the moon? Ha, Ha! You are silly!'

'Dad says I'm stupid,' said Frankie. Alphonsine stopped laughing and frowned. 'He says I'm a failure. "F"-for-Frankie. "F"-for-failure.'

'Ha! Your dad, he knows nothing,' scoffed Alphonsine, '"F" is for Fearless! "F" is for Fantastic!' But Frankie just looked at his feet. Alphonsine leaned forward and tweaked the end of Frankie's nose. 'Sometimes we must resist,' she said, 'sometimes we must say, "Stop! Zat is enough! I am not afraid of you!"'

CHAPTER THREE
FAILURE IS NOT AN OPTION

Mr Blewitt was grinning like a chimp when he came home from work. 'My pretty pumpkin!' he called to his wife who was crouched on the floor doing her exercises, 'My honey-bee! I think I have cracked our problem.'

'What problem, darling?' grunted Mrs Blewitt as she tucked her left foot behind her head.

'Our horrid, grubby little problem, our squirty little embarassment, our eight-year-old itch!'

'Oh, you mean Frankie. Could you get the other foot?' Mr Blewitt twisted his wife's right foot behind her neck, so she looked like a strange sort of crab. 'I've been so compleeeetely stressed darling, just look at the lines on my forehead! Tell me, what is it?'

'Boarding school,' announced Mr Blewitt proudly, brandishing a brochure, 'The finest in the country. They'll get rid of all that rubbish he keeps between his ears, just you wait and see.'

'How simply fabulous!' Mrs Blewitt trilled.

'It's called Crammar Grammar,' Mr Blewitt continued, 'and it's run by a Dr Calus Gore. Proper egghead. Listen to this.' Mr Blewitt read out loud from the brochure, '"Are you spending a fortune on your child's schooling but getting no results? You deserve better. At Crammar Grammar we use the most advanced learning techniques to stretch your children far beyond their limits." It's just what Frankie needs! We've been spoiling the little blighter for much too long!'

'It sounds delightful!' chirped Mrs Blewitt, 'What a clever chap you are!' Mr Blewitt puffed up like a toad.

'Frankie will have to pass an exam and then there's an interview with the headmaster. They have to check that we are the right sort of people. Royalty go to this place you know.'

'How simply maaarvellous,' gasped Mrs Blewitt. 'But we can't have Frankie...' she lowered her voice to a whisper, '*failing*! I could never show my face at the Country Club again!'

'Don't worry, my crumpet,' said Mr Blewitt. 'Failure is not an option.'

'Ooooh, I love it when you say that,' giggled Mrs Blewitt then, losing her balance, she toppled on to her back like an upturned beetle.

Failure was *never* an option for Mr Blewitt. When he wanted something – well, he jolly well went out and grabbed it, and this time he wanted to send Frankie to Crammar Grammar. Not satisfied with throwing out Frankie's toys, Mr Blewitt decided to pay a procession of tutors to give him extra lessons. So, as you can imagine, in the weeks before his Crammar Grammar entrance exam there was no playtime, no mucking about and definitely no toys for Frankie Blewitt. As soon as he got home from a long day of classes he had to do an hour of reading with Miss Muster, who looked as if she'd been stacked on a library shelf for a hundred years, followed by an hour of Chinese with Miss Tang, who was as sweet as a lychee but impossible to understand, and after that, two long hours of sums with Mr Bellicosi, who smelled of cheese and had a terrible temper. By the time the tutors left it was far too late to think about adventures and besides, Frankie was so tired he would fall asleep before he had reached the top of the stairs.

After a few weeks of this gruelling routine, Frankie was so exhausted he even forgot about his birthday. I mean, can you imagine forgetting your own birthday? That's how tired he was. It was only when he saw a pile of presents on the kitchen table that he remembered he had just turned nine. Frankie rubbed his eyes in disbelief.

'Are they for me?' he asked cautiously, hardly believing his luck.

'Don't say we never get you anything,' muttered Mr Blewitt, his head buried in his newspaper. Frankie could hardly contain his excitement.

'Oh, Wow!' he cried as he tore back the wrapping paper. Would he get a sledge perhaps, or a telescope, or a game to play with his friends? Frankie was just dying to go out and play. But as the paper dropped to the floor, Frankie's heart sank. All he found was a big, heavy pile of books with no pictures.

'That should keep you out of trouble!' snorted Mr Blewitt. 'You can start with the dictionary. I want everything from Aardvark to Axe memorised by tomorrow.'

'They're great, Dad,' said Frankie, trying to hide his disappointment. Heaving the books off the table, he trudged upstairs to his bedroom and opened the first volume of the dictionary.

'Aardvark... abacus... abolish...' Frankie tried reading out loud to keep himself awake, but he was so tired the letters didn't stay still on the page.

'Abysmal... accident...' Frankie yawned and rubbed his eyes, 'acid... advanced...' He glanced at the clock, but the hands seemed to have stopped moving, 'Advantage... adventure... Adventure!' Frankie sighed. What a brilliant word. It made him think of jungles and monsters and heroes and heroines and knights in armour! As he stared at the vast grey pages, his mind began to trip and somersault and wander off on its own. Slowly, the words transformed into rows of soldiers, and the paragraphs became armies, facing each other across the pages. All of a sudden, Frankie found himself in the midst of a blazing battle. 'Raise the drawbridge men!' he shouted to his troops. Then, using everything he could lay his hands on, Frankie began to build a fortress. The books made sturdy bricks, and tubes of wrapping paper made for some splendid turrets. 'Hold steady!' he shouted, 'The enemy is approaching!' Then, just as he was shielding himself from a hail of arrows, Frankie heard a roaring noise above him. *'Dragons!'*

But there were no dragons. Looking up, Frankie saw his father reaching down towards

him over the pile of books. He seized Frankie's collar with his huge hand, lifted him clear off the ground and fixed him with his mean little eyes.

'Do you think I pay hundreds of hard-earned pounds...?!' he started, but Frankie didn't hear the rest. He felt a twisting in his stomach, and a prickling in his cheeks, and heard a buzzing in his ears. Then, before he knew what he was doing, he stared right back at his dad and shouted 'STOP! THAT'S ENOUGH! I AM NOT AFRAID OF YOU!' Mr Blewitt was so surprised at Frankie's outburst that he dropped him like a hot crumpet. Frankie was stunned. He had expected his dad to turn red and start shouting, but no, Mr Blewitt wasn't used to being stood up to. He was completely stumped. He stood for a moment with his mouth hanging open like a gibbon. Then turned and stomped out of the room, slamming the door behind him.

'I am not afraid,' Frankie repeated to himself as he picked himself up and started to rebuild his fortress, book by book, 'I am NOT afraid.' And, you know what? For the first time ever, he wasn't afraid. Frankie Blewitt was fed up with being shouted at and pushed about and locked up with books when all his friends were outside playing. He'd had enough of being called a nitwit and a numbskull and a failure. *I'm fed up with it*, he thought to himself, *Alphonsine is right. It is time to resist!* He strapped a large book to his chest like a big plate of armour and took up his position behind the battlements.

'I am Fantastic Frankie!' he shouted, 'and I am ready for ADVENTURE!'

CHAPTER FOUR
THE PARACHUTE

When Alphonsine heard what Frankie had told his dad she laughed so hard her eye popped out and rolled into the washing-up. 'HOO HOO! HEE HEE!' she hooted as Colette dived into the bubbles to fetch it. Alphonsine gave the eyeball a shake, squished it back into its socket and studied Frankie closely. 'I am proud. Yes, very proud of you.'

'Tell me more about the Resistance, Alfie,' said Frankie. 'Tell me about your adventures.'

'First things first,' said Alphonsine, throwing Frankie a frying pan. 'Pancakes!'

'It is 1942. Right in the middle of the war,' Alphonsine began, once the pancakes were on the table, 'I am in the garden, hanging out ze washing, when I hear a voice. "Excusay-mwa? Excuse me?" it says. I spin round ready to clobber this trespasser with my washing basket. But there is no danger. Instead there is a young man in googles hanging upside-down in my apple-tree.'

'Goggles,' said Frankie through a mouthful of pancake.

'Yes, googles, zat is what I said. "Mademoiselle," says the young man, "I am British. Bree-tan-eek. Can you help me please?" And I look, and I see that he is tangled up in the cords of a big silk parachute. Straight away I understand. The Royal Air Force drop him out of a plane during the night and a wind pick him up and dump him in my garden. I am cross, of course, because he has bended the branches of my tree, but I get the scissors and cut him down.' Alphonsine helped herself to another pancake.

'Is that it?' asked Frankie, who was hoping for a bit more action.

'But of course not,' Alphonsine spluttered. 'There was a British person in my apple tree! If the Nasties found out, they would squash us both like flies.' Alphonsine squished a sultana with the back of her fork, so Frankie could see how very nasty this would be. 'I had to hide him quick, quick. So I clean out the coal bunker in the garden, give him a blanket and shove him inside. He stays there for weeks. I feed him, I talk to him, but always very quiet in case there are sticky noses about.'

'Sticky noses?' asked Frankie.

'Yes, yes. People who are always sticking in their noses, poking about, nosy pokers.'

'Nosy Parkers,' corrected Frankie.

43

'Yes, yes. You want to hear the story or not?'

Frankie nodded energetically.

'But there are sticky pokers everywhere. One day somebody snitches on me to the Nasties and before I know it – *Bash! Bash! Bash!* – there is somebody at the door.

'I lock the coal bunker, put the key on a chain around my neck and go to see who is it. But when I walk into the kitchen, there are already two officers, one fat as a pudding, one bony as a bird, poking about in my cupboards. "Ve hear you have a Visitor." says the fat one, helping himself to my biscuits. "No officer," I say, "No visitors." But they do not believe. Straight away they start turning the place outside-in looking for the parachuter. They look in the cupboards and under the bed and behind the chairs, but they do not find. They are about to give up and go away when the bony one catches me looking towards the garden and straight away he suspects. "Aha!" he says, "Ze Visitor is perhaps in ze Garden, no? Perhaps in ze Coal Bunker?"

"'Ah Ya!" says the fat one, "Coal Bunkers is the favourish hiding place of Parachuters!" My heart is still as a stone. What will I do, what will I do, I ask myself, as the officers try to break open the bunker.

"'Vere is the Key?!" they shout, and I say, "I do not know, I do not have it." But again they do not believe. "I think she is fibbing," says the fat one. "Vot do you think? Do you think she is fibbing?"

"'Ah Ya, definitely a Fibber," says the bony one. "So vot do ve do?" shouts fatty. "Ve make her talk, yes, yes, ve make her talk," he says and then he reaches into his pocket and takes out a little green pill. Straight away I feel sick to the bones.'

'What was it?' asked Frankie. 'What was in the pill? Poison?'

'Worse! It was a Telitol Tablet. A filthy little pill that makes you tell the truth, whether you like it or not. You swallow and suddenly you start blabbing. And you can do nothing to stop. All your deepest darkest secrets, they are shooting out of your mouth. I was afraid I would tell them where was the key and then it would be squashing all round.' Frankie looked at the sultana and shuddered. 'But lucky for me the Resistance taught me a clever trick. When they put the pill in my mouth, I twist my tongue like so,' Alphonsine opened her mouth wide and twisted her tongue right round like a pretzel. 'I stick the pill between my gums and my cheek. Then I pretend to gulp it down.' Frankie picked a sultana out of his pancake and tried to do the same. 'I pretend to eat the pill so that the officers think I will tell them the truth. Then I point at the apple tree and I say, "Listen very carefully, the key is in zat hole in ze tree." But

I must look nervy because they is still suspicious.

'"You better not be telling a whopper!" says the fatsome one, slitting his eyes, "You know what happens when people tell us whoppers." I knows what happens when people tell whoppers to the Nasties and I is very, very afraid. But I have one more trick. The most important trick the Resistance taught me. The tip-top secret trick.'

'What is it?' said Frankie, 'What's the secret trick?'

'When you is very, very afraid,' she whispered, 'When somebody make you so scared that your knees is knocking and your feet is sweating and your ears is ringing, you close your eyes and you think of that person...' Alphonsine glanced over her shoulder, in case anybody should be listening, and whispered, '...with their pants on their head.' Frankie spluttered with laughter, but Alphonsine was completely serious. 'The pants-on-head trick is the most important, the most noblest weapon of the Resistance! Pants-on-head makes you see that bullies is, in fact, wallies! Pants-on-head gives you COURAGE.' Frankie stifled his giggles. 'So,' Alphonsine continued, sucking on a sultana, 'I imagine these two Nasty officers with their knickers over their ears and I take a deep breath, and I say with perfect calm, "Yes. The key is in zat hole." Straight away they believe and rush over to my tree. The bony bird is standing on his tippy-toes trying to get a peek, and the fat pudding is sticking his arm in the hole and feeling about for the key. "I have it!" he shouts and pulls out his hand. But between his fingers is not a key. Between his fingers is something black and yellow and very, very angry. In the tree is not a key. In the tree is a WASP NEST!'

'What happened next?' asked Frankie, on the edge of his chair.

'Well, what do you think?' said Alphonsine, 'They run and they scream and they wave their arms in the air. But this makes the wasps even madder and straight away they start stinging the officers all over their botties. *Oh la la!* They are making such a noise that the whole village comes out to see what is the bother. Of course the wasp is a pesky little beast, and it is getting inside the officers' uniforms. So what do they do? They start pulling off the boots and the jacket and the trouser till they is stark-bottom naked!'

'Hoo hoo hoo!' Frankie was laughing so hard he almost choked on his pancake.

'Yes, it was very hilarious,' said Alphonsine, licking a last blob of chocolate sauce off her finger. 'Those Nasties NEVER bother me again!'

'What happened to the parachutist?' asked Frankie, coughing up a sultana.

'Oh, him,' Alphonsine picked her teeth and

shifted in her seat, 'I marry him.'

'Really?' said Frankie, who had no idea that Alphonsine had been married.

'But of course! We was happy as pigeons. I make my wedding dress out of the silk parachute, and after the war we come to England and open a chemist shop. He was a brilliant chemist...' Alphonsine looked down at her empty plate, and Frankie noticed a tear in the corner of her eye. She quickly wiped it away and began to clear the table. 'But zat is another story.'

'YOOHOO! FRANKIE! Mummy's been to the shops!' Mrs Blewitt burst into the kitchen grinning so ferociously Frankie thought her face would split. She was wearing what looked like a string of golfballs round her neck and on her feet were a snappy pair of crocodile-skin shoes. 'Don't you just *adore* the pearls?' she crooned, twiddling her necklace between perfectly shaped fingernails.

'I deserve a little treat. I deserve a little me-time.' Frankie wasn't listening. He had noticed a tuft of fur poking out of the largest shopping bag and was gingerly peeking inside. 'DON'T TOUCH!' screeched Mrs Blewitt, snatching the bag away from him. Then, as if she were lifting a sleeping child, she hauled out a glamorous fur coat. 'It's for your big day!' she whispered, as if she might wake it up, 'I want to make a special effort.' She slipped the coat over her shoulders and flounced about the kitchen like a huge, scary hamster.

'What big day?' asked Frankie suspiciously as his mother skipped out of the door to fetch more shopping bags.

'Your interview at Crammar Grammar of course!' she shouted. 'Didn't your daddy tell you? We're sending you to boarding school!'

CHAPTER FIVE
THE SUIT

'Boarding school! Wow!' said Frankie, 'Isn't that great Alphonsine?!' But Alphonsine had turned as white as a goose. *'Oh la la,'* she muttered, *'Oh la la la la!'* Frankie didn't understand why Alphonsine was so upset, 'I'll write to you all the time,' he told her, 'I'll come and visit.'

'No, my little cabbage, you do not understand,' Frankie noticed that her hands were shaking, 'Crammar Grammar is a terrible place. TE-REE-BLE!' Frankie hesitated. He had never seen Alphonsine in such a state.

53

'It can't be worse than living here,' he joked.

'Yes, worse! Much worser! Listen very carefully. Three years ago my friend Yvonne worked for a family, the father, he was mad as a monkey, and the mother she was loopy as a caterpillar. They had a nice little boy, same age as you, and they pushed him off to this dreadful place, this... Crammar Grammar,' Alphonsine mopped her forehead with her apron, 'I do not know what they did to him there, but he has never been the same since, NEVER!'

'Fraaaaaankie darling!' yelled Mrs Blewitt from upstairs, 'I have something for you! For your big day!' Frankie paused and looked at Alphonsine.

'Go on, little cabbage,' she said, 'there is time.'

Mrs Blewitt held up a small grey suit. She didn't often buy Frankie clothes. In fact his jeans had become so small that he had to tug them down at the ankles to hide his socks. So, at first, Frankie was rather pleased to be getting something new to wear. But he struggled to get into the itchy trousers and the shiny black shoes pinched his toes.

'Stop wriggling!' hissed Mrs Blewitt as she pulled a tie around his throat. Frankie glanced at his reflection in the mirror. He certainly looked very smart, but he felt horribly uncomfortable. The jacket was as stiff as a cornflakes packet and the collar squeezed his neck. Frankie wiggled about to loosen the sleeves. 'Stop it!' shrieked Mrs Blewitt, pulling his ears. 'Do you have any idea how spectacularly expensive that suit is?!' Mrs Blewitt breathed in deeply through her nostrils. 'When the headmaster sees you in it, he won't care that you are...' she pursed her lips as if she was going to spit out something particularly disgusting, *failing at school*. He'll see that we are

the right sort of people… and *that's* what matters!'
But Frankie was hardly listening. He saw something
strangely familiar in his reflection. Something in
the stiff shoulders of the jacket perhaps, or was it
in the shine of his shoes? Frankie couldn't put his
finger on it. Then, all of a sudden, there it was.
Mrs Blewitt sighed and patted Frankie on the
head. 'You look just like your father.' she said.

Frankie felt as if he
were about to choke.
His mum was
right. He looked
just like his
dad. Frankie
pulled off his
tie as if it
were a boa
constrictor,
kicked off

his shiny shoes and, deaf to Mrs Blewitt's screeches, ran off to find Alphonsine. Whatever this Crammar Grammar place was, one thing was for sure. Frankie did NOT want to go there. He had to find a way out, and fast. Frankie swung round the banister, charged down the stairs, and WHUMP! ran straight into Mr Blewitt who had just got back from work.

'What the devil...?!' bellowed Mr Blewitt as Frankie rebounded off his chest and went sprawling on to the floor.

'I don't want to go! I don't want to go!' yelled Frankie in panic.

'What are you talking about?'

'I don't want to go to Crammar Grammar!' Frankie shouted. Mr Blewitt towered over Frankie like a smouldering volcano.

'Don't want to go to Crammar Grammar?' he sneered. Frankie knew when his dad was serious, and this time he was as serious as a tombstone. 'Now, you'd better get your act together my son,' he spat, 'and it had better happen fast, because, like it or not, you are going to that interview.' Mr Blewitt leaned right down and pushed his face close to Frankie's. 'And you are going to that school.' Then, shoving Frankie aside with the edge of his foot, he thudded up the stairs.

Frankie felt like a small stinky pile of rubbish. He slowly picked himself up and sloped off to find Alphonsine, who was hosing down her motorbike outside.

'What am I going to do, Alfie?' he said, plonking himself down on the grass. 'I don't want to go, I don't want to be like my dad. But I have no choice.' Alphonsine shook her head.

'There is ALWAYS a choice, little cabbage,' she said. 'Always a choice. Resistance is not easy-peasy-pip-squeak! It is most difficult. MUCH more difficult than times-tables.' Frankie knew she was right, but he just couldn't see how he could get out of his interview at Crammar Grammar. If he ran away his dad would catch him, and if he messed up the interview on purpose his dad would know. Either way would be his dad's way in the end.

Frankie noticed that Colette was sitting on the porch looking most put out.

'What's wrong with Colette?'

'Ah. She has the flea,' said Alphonsine. 'But shhh! She is embarrassed.' Frankie glanced sideways at the poodle, who was scratching furiously behind her ear. 'It is not ladylike,' said Alphonsine, 'She hate it. She refuse to come to the shop with me.'

'Really...' murmured Frankie, and a brilliant idea began to take shape in his mind. A really brilliant idea.

'I've got it!' he cried, leaping to his feet, 'I've got it!'

'Ah well, ze flea is catching,' Alphonsine replied absent-mindedly.

'No, not fleas. I've got a plan! To stop them sending me to Crammar Grammar!' Alphonsine turned off the hose and smiled.

'You have? I knew you would!'

'Yes,' said Frankie, 'but I need Colette's help.'

'Of course,' replied Alphonsine, 'Colette is at your service. What is it she must do?'

That night, worn out by all her itching and scratching, Colette was delighted to settle down to sleep in a nice warm basket, thoughtfully lined with Mrs Blewitt's new fur coat.

CHAPTER SIX
MR WALLET

Mrs Blewitt always took hours to get ready. On the morning of the interview, Frankie sat on the sofa and watched as the poor hairdresser restyled his mum's hair for the tenth time in three hours. 'You have to tell these people!' Mrs Blewitt sighed to Frankie once the exhausted hairdresser had left. 'All I ask for is perfection. Is that so unreasonable?' She took her new fur coat from the wardrobe, where Frankie had placed it earlier that morning, and slipped it over her shoulders. 'Faaaaaaaabulous!' she purred at her reflection in the mirror, then glanced at her watch and squawked.

As they screeched down the drive in his mum's sports car, Frankie wondered how long it would be before his plan took effect. He had rather hoped it would work straight away, but Mrs Blewitt didn't seem to have noticed anything unusual. Frankie crossed his fingers. His plan had to work. If it didn't, it was Crammar Grammar for sure.

'We'll take a detour through the Country Club,' announced Mrs Blewitt, opening the top of the car so everybody could get a look at her fancy hairdo, 'I'd like to say a quick hello to the girls.'

Now the Country Club was not, as you might think, for people with tractors – heavens no! The Country Club was exclusively for ever-so-rich, ever-so-snooty types like the Blewitts. The clubhouse was a vast mansion designed to look like a roman villa, with great big columns and a fountain that had a statue of a little boy peeing in it. The peeing fountain had always been a bit of a mystery to Frankie – if *he* ever widdled in the swimming pool he'd get a clip round the ear. But this morning Frankie had more important things to worry about. Mrs Blewitt parked the car next to the terrace where her friends, Filly and Fenella, were sipping cocktails after a tennis match.

'How maaaaaarvellous to see you,' drawled Filly, as Mrs Blewitt stepped out of the car like a Hollywood actress. Fenella looked Mrs Blewitt up and down enviously then forced a smile,

'Aren't you hot in that coat, sweetie?' she chirruped.

'Not at all,' shrilled Mrs Blewitt, striking a pose, 'besides, as they say in Paris, one must suffer to be beautiful.' The ladies threw back their heads and laughed.

'Ah ha ha ha ha…!'

Suddenly, Mrs Blewitt froze rigid. Frankie

held his breath as her eyes began to bulge and her lips twitched in discomfort.

'Are you all right, darling?' asked Filly, peering over her sunglasses.

'Perfect,' strained Mrs Blewittt through clenched teeth, 'I'm simply perffff—' Mrs Blewitt couldn't contain herself any longer. She pulled off a glove and vigorously scratched the side of her neck. Then she scratched the other side. Then she scratched her scalp, and her arms and her armpit, then both armpits at the same time.

'Whatever is the matter?!' shrieked Fenella.

'Ooh Ooh! Ah Ah!' cried Mrs Blewitt, leaping about like an ape and scratching herself all over. Frankie bit his knuckles to stopper a giggle as everyone at the Country Club gathered around to see what the jiminy had got into Mrs Blewitt.

'She's completely bonkers,' hissed a woman with a tiny dog in her handbag.

'Barking!' agreed another.

Mrs Blewitt's skin was itching so ferociously that, for the first time in her life, she couldn't have given two hoots what anyone thought. 'Give me that!' she growled, grabbing Fenella's tennis racquet. And, before Fenella had the chance to complain, Mrs Blewitt started scratching her back with the head, 'Ooooh that's better! Ahhhhh!'

'Darling!' shrieked Filly, pointing at Mrs Blewitt in horror, 'What are those THINGS on your coat?'

'What things?!' Mrs Blewitt glanced at her shoulder. 'EEEEEEE!' she hollered, running in circles. Courtesy of Colette the poodle, Mrs Blewitt's coat was alive with fleas. 'Heeeelp! Heeeeeeelp!' she screamed, waving her hands in the air. But nobody moved a muscle. Whatever Mrs Blewitt had, nobody else wanted it. Besides, nothing this entertaining had been seen at the

Club for years. There was only one thing for it. Mrs Blewitt charged towards the fountain like a crazed wildebeest and hurled herself in.

KERSPLASH!

Mrs Blewitt hit the water with such force that Filly and Fenella were soaked from head to toe and ran squelching into the clubhouse. Mrs Blewitt sat dazed in the fountain. Her new fur coat looked like something you'd pull out of the plughole, but she was so relieved the itching had stopped that she just didn't care. 'You can forget about the interview Frankie,' she gurgled, as the fountain sprinkled playfully on her hairdo. 'We're going home.'

Frankie gazed at the sky as his mum drove away from the Country Club. He'd done it! He was saved! He felt happy and triumphant – like he could do anything. But, with his head in the clouds and the wind whistling in his ears, he didn't hear his mum make a very important phone call. 'It was ghastly darling!' Mrs Blewitt blubbed to her husband, 'I'm traumatised, quite traumatised!'

'That son of ours is behind this,' Mr Blewitt's voice crackled back, 'I can smell it. The slippery little eel has been acting up for weeks. But he can't fool me. Don't you fret my popsicle! I will put plan B into action and there is NOTHING Frankie can do about it. As I like to say; if at first you don't succeed – flash the cash!'

When Mr Blewitt got back from work, he looked as smug as a crocodile. 'Where's your mother?' he bellowed at Frankie, 'I have some excellent news.' Once he had everyone's attention, Mr Blewitt poured himself a drink and began. 'Everything is fixed!' he announced, 'I twisted a few arms, bent a few ears and got the job done.' He paused for effect and took a manly swig of whisky. 'Frankie is off to Crammar Grammar!' Mrs Blewitt clapped her hands with glee, 'Term starts tomorrow so you can start packing your bags.'

'But that's impossible,' cried Frankie in dismay, 'I missed my interview!'

'Doesn't matter,' snorted Mr Blewitt. 'I paid a little visit to the headmaster myself. He's a good chap, knows what's what. Besides...' Mr Blewitt pulled some banknotes out of his back pocket and waved them in Frankie's face, 'Nobody says no to Mr Wallet! Ha ha! The sooner you learn that the better!'

'Ha ha! Ha ha ha ha ha!' Mr and Mrs Blewitt fell about laughing. 'Nobody says no to Mr Wallet! Ha ha ha!' Frankie felt sick. It was too late to think up another plan. He was off to Crammar Grammar and that was the end of it.

The next morning Frankie packed his suitcase and went downstairs, where a taxi was waiting. Alphonsine gave him a big hug and Colette licked his hand.

'Listen very carefully,' said Alphonsine, slipping something cold and metallic around his neck. 'This is a dog whistle. It make a noise zat is too high for humans, but Colette will hear. If ever you are in danger, you blow on this as hard as you can, and I come and get you. You understand little cabbage?' Frankie nodded and hugged her tightly.

'Stop dawdling Frankie!' shouted Mr Blewitt, pushing him into the back of the taxi, 'There'll be none of your funny business at Crammar Grammar. I'll tell you that for free. And remember,' Mr Blewitt slammed the door and pushed his face against the window, 'failure...' he snarled, 'is not an option.' As the taxi sped away Frankie waved frantically to Alphonsine out of the back window.

But she didn't see him. She was too busy trying to hold back Colette who was barking wildly after the car.

Finally the house disappeared from view, and Frankie turned round in his seat to look at the road ahead. He felt very alone and very scared. In fact, he had never felt so very alone and so very scared in his whole nine years. But somewhere, deep in his belly, he also felt a twinge of something else, something thrilling. He took a deep breath, pulled himself upright in his seat and whispered, 'I am not afraid. I am Fantastic Frankie and this is my first adventure!'

CHAPTER SEVEN
CRAMMAR GRAMMAR

The taxi dumped Frankie in the middle of a vast stone courtyard. This was it; Crammar Grammar.

It looks like a prison, thought Frankie as he gazed up at the old blackened walls that surrounded him on every side. They were so high, and so solid it felt as if they could move in at any moment and squash him flat. Frankie swallowed nervously. 'No wonder Alfie didn't want me to come here,' he murmured. 'It's horrible.' The narrow windows frowned down on him as if they could read his mind and a shudder passed through his body as the iron gates clanked shut. 'Nothing to be afraid of,' he told himself. But he felt like a tiny mouse in a huge, dark trap.

Crammar Grammar was completely still and utterly silent. Not a breath of life stirred. Not a bird, not a leaf, not even the wind. In fact, it was so silent that all Frankie could hear was the blood pulsing in his ears. He was just beginning to hope that he had come to the wrong place when...

'AAAAAGH!' He felt a hand on his shoulder. The walls shrieked back at Frankie as he spun around to see who or what had crept up on him.

'Oh, dear. I *am* sorry,' said a tiny, white-haired gentleman who looked even more startled than Frankie himself. 'I didn't mean to alarm you. I'm the porter here at Crammar Grammar. You looked a little lost, so I thought I could show you to your class. You are one of the new first years, aren't you?' The gentleman was neatly buttoned into a

jacket and cap and reminded Frankie of a smart toy soldier.

'Oh, right, yes, sorry,' stammered Frankie, whose heart was pounding so hard that he could see his shirt moving. The porter hoisted Frankie's trunk on to his back and signalled for Frankie to follow him.

'I can carry that,' offered Frankie, afraid that the old man's knees would snap beneath the weight. But the gentleman wouldn't hear of it and marched ahead like a valiant ant.

'No trouble at all, Master...'

'Blewitt. Frankie Blewitt.'

'Delighted to meet you Master Blewitt,' said the gentleman as they walked through the main entrance and into a dark maze of corridors, 'I would gladly tell you my name too. But I've forgotten it.' Frankie was astonished. He often forgot to do his homework or brush his teeth, but he'd never heard of somebody forgetting their name.

'How did you forget?' Frankie asked.

'Oh, I can't remember,' said the porter, blinking his cloudy blue eyes, 'I can't remember much these days. Only the important things like always say please and thank you, never speak with your mouth full and tea should be taken at four o'clock sharp. Apart from that it's in one ear and out the other. But never mind all that. It's your first day at school. I should think you're a bit nervous.'

'A bit,' Frankie admitted.

'No need,' said the porter kindly. 'In fact your timing is impeccable. Only yesterday, I overheard the headmaster saying he has big plans for this place.'

'Really?' said Frankie.

'Oh, yes. He said he would put this school on the map. Crammar Grammar, he said, would become the most… the most… um… now what did he say?' The porter frowned in concentration, 'I'm afraid I've forgotten the rest. But I imagine you'll find out soon enough.' They stopped in front of a closed door and the porter knocked smartly. 'Now this is where the first years are, so in you go Master… um…'

'Blewitt, Frankie Blewitt.'

'Yes, of course. Well, good luck Master Blewitt.'

Frankie was just starting to hope that Crammar Grammar would be full of friendly types like the porter, when a very unfriendly fist grabbed his collar and pulled him into the classroom.

'The exam started half an hour ago,' growled a grim-faced teenager with a prefect badge.

'Wow,' said Frankie, 'exams already?'

'Exams always,' the prefect sneered, and plonked him at a spare desk. Frankie glanced around the classroom. It wasn't anything like his old school. At his old school, the walls were covered with colourful paintings and maps and poems written by the class. But here the walls were utterly bare, and there wasn't even a window to stare out of. In fact, as Frankie noted to his surprise, all the windows had been bricked up on purpose. But strangest of all was the silence. There was no giggling or whispering, no 'Please, Sir, can I go to the loo?' just a furious scratching of pens. Frankie looked around at his new classmates, hoping to catch someone's eye, but they were all hunched over their exam papers with worried looks on their faces.

'Exams it is then,' sighed Frankie and opened his paper. His heart sank. The questions were so difficult, Frankie felt sure they had all been taken from a book called *Things Frankie Blewitt Does Not Know*. Things like, what is the capital of Chile? Frankie scratched his head; he knew the capital of

England and the capital of Scotland. But Chile?' As he was chewing his pencil and wondering if it had anything to do with chilli-con-carne, he noticed that the girl at the next table was not writing at all. In fact, her head was on the desk and she looked like she was fast asleep. Frankie prodded her with a ruler.

'Wha—!' The girl sat up quickly and glanced about her, 'Where am I? What's going on?'

'You're in an exam,' said Frankie. The girl sat bolt upright and blinked her eyes in terror. Then, to Frankie's surprise, she gave a quiet whimper and slumped back down on the desk. Frankie prodded her again.

'Are you okay?' he whispered. The girl jumped to attention once more, and glanced about her wildly.

'You have to write something down,' said Frankie, trying to be helpful. 'It's an exam.' But before he could say any more, *DONK*, the girl's head landed back on the desk. Frankie prodded her again, and again, trying to keep her awake, but every time the girl heard the word 'Exam' her eyes would bulge with fright, and she would go out like a candle. By the end of the hour neither of them had written a single word.

'Oh, dear. Oh, no. I've messed it up again,' she squeaked, as the prefect collected in the papers.

'You kept falling asleep,' said Frankie.

'I know,' she replied, 'I can't help it. Every time I hear *that word*, I get a funny feeling in my belly. Then everything goes dark and I pass out. It's like somebody pulls the plug and *zzzp* – game over. I never get good marks.'

'Me neither,' said Frankie. The girl smiled.

'My name's Anita,' she said, 'But everyone calls me Neet. What's yours?'

By the time they had walked to the dining hall, Frankie and Neet had become best friends. Neet's parents sounded just about as crazy as Mr and Mrs Blewitt and all of her sisters had been sent to Crammar Grammar before her. In fact, Neet came from a long line of Crammar Grammarians. Her mum had been to Crammar Grammar, and her mum's mum, and even her mum's mum's mum, and every single one of them had been head girl.

'Look.' Neet pointed to a polished board on the dining room wall. The board displayed the names of former head-girls in fine gold lettering.

'Ameena Banerjee, Asha Banerjee, Anisha Banerjee,' Frankie read.

'Right,' said Neet. 'And if I'm not next on the list, Mum will go bananas.'

'Your mum sounds just like my dad,' said Frankie. 'You know, I'm glad to get away from my parents. Nothing could be worse than living at home... Right, Neet?' But Neet just stared at Frankie with a look of utter astonishment. 'Nobody's told you about this place, have they?' she said.

CHAPTER EIGHT
ANITA BANERJEE

The advantage of coming from a long line of Crammar Grammarians is that you have some idea of what to expect. Anita Banerjee was new to Crammar Grammar, but compared with Frankie she was an expert. As they waited in the dinner queue, Neet told Frankie everything she knew. 'The one to watch...' she dropped her voice to a whisper, 'is Dr Gore.'

Neet was right of course. Crammar Grammar had never been a bundle of fun but when Dr Gore became headmaster things went from bad to

worse. Then they went from worse to *even* worse
– and that was very bad indeed. The trouble was,
Dr Gore didn't give a bean about children. In fact,
given the choice between a bean and a nine-year-
old, Dr Gore would pick the bean every time. Why?
Because Dr Gore wasn't really a teacher at all. He
was a scientist by profession and a very brainy one
too. As a young man he had wanted to be the
brainiest, most talked-about scientist in the world.
But, unfortunately for him, he never made the Big
Discovery that earned him the fame and fortune
he thought he deserved. Other scientists had put
men on the moon, cured ghastly diseases or had
found the answer to some impossible sum. But,
despite years of sweating away in laboratories, Dr
Gore never made the breakthrough that would
truly reveal his genius.

'I don't see what all that's got to do with us,'
said Frankie as a dinner lady with a face like an

angry cabbage plopped a pile of peas on to his plate and drenched them in fish oil.

'It has everything to do with us,' whispered Neet, but Frankie was so horrified by the greenish goo that he had stopped listening.

'Is there anything else to eat?' Frankie asked, trying to hide his disgust.

'Noooooo!' growled the dinner lady through a mouthful of something that looked like sponge cake, 'just peeeeeeeeas!' Frankie thought he might be sick.

'The thing is, Frankie,' Neet continued as they found themselves a table, 'Dr Gore hasn't given up. He's still trying to make his Big Discovery.'

'What do you mean?' said Frankie, prodding at his food.

'Well, the thing is…'

'Bleeeeeeuuuuuurgh! That is HORRIBLE!' Frankie spluttered through his peas. 'That is the

WORST thing I have ever tasted! Urrrrrrrgh!'

'Course it is,' said Neet, trying to force down a mouthful. 'It's all part of Dr Gore's experiment.'

'What experiment?' said Frankie, rinsing his mouth out with a glass of water.

'That's what I'm trying to tell you, Frankie,' said Neet. 'Other scientists experiment on guinea-pigs or rats, but Dr Gore has something much better.' Frankie hoped he hadn't heard right. He stopped fussing over his food and looked Neet in the eye.

'You don't mean...?'

Neet nodded, 'That's right. Crammar Grammar is Dr Gore's laboratory and we are the lab-rats.' Frankie couldn't believe what he was hearing.

'But he can't experiment on *us*!' Frankie whispered. 'Why doesn't somebody stop him?!'

Neet shook her head. 'Who? Our parents? They're Dr Gore's biggest fans. The trouble is the headmaster wants to turn us all into prodigies. You know, children with brains like calculators. He thinks that if he can turn kids like us into proper brain-boxes, everyone will think he is the best scientist that ever lived. My mum reckons he's a genius.'

'But I don't want a brain like a calculator!' Frankie stammered.

'Look around you,' Neet continued. 'This whole place has been designed to make us cleverer. No playtime, lessons all weekend, oily peas for lunch. They might taste like snot, but they're good for the brain.' Frankie stared at his plate in horror. So this was why his parents had sent him here; to turn him into a prodigy. Then they could show him off to their friends at the Country Club. Frankie could see it now. 'That's my boy!' his dad would say, 'A true Blewitt!'

Frankie glanced towards a table of seniors.

They looked tired and grey, as if they had been collecting dust for years. 'They're the normal ones,' said Neet. 'Some of them go completely nuts. My sister Asha reckons that every now and then, Dr Gore gets the dinner lady to put stuff in somebody's food. Stuff that messes with their heads.'

'What, like potions?'

'That sort of thing. Stuff to make us smarter. But sometimes it doesn't work properly, or people have funny reactions. There was this girl in the sixth form who started speaking Latin all the time. Nobody knew what she was on about. Then there was this boy who started rhyming all his words. He couldn't help it. He'd say, "Nice to see you, vicar," then, "are you wearing frilly knickers?" stuff like that. It gave him a massive headache.'

'We have to get out of here!' Frankie urged. But Neet just shook her head.

'And go where?' she said. 'My parents would just send me straight back.' Frankie looked down at his dinner plate. He knew his would too.

'Then we have to do something,' he said. 'We have to stop him!' Neet stared at Frankie, wide-eyed.

'No. You don't want to cross Dr Gore,' she said shaking her head rapidly. 'It's much too risky. You never know what he'll do to you. There was this boy, Bobby Chan. Dr Gore caught him with a contraband comic and he made him balance the whole of the *Encyclopaedia Britannica* on his head for ten hours.'

'Ow!' said Frankie, rubbing his scalp.

'You bet! He shrank twenty centimetres and his head has never been the same shape since. But there's worse.' Neet glanced over her shoulder then leaned in closer, 'If you make him really mad, he throws you in the Hole.'

The headmaster went to great lengths to invent the strangest and most ingenious punishments for his students, but the Hole was his pride and joy. Its beauty was its simplicity. There were no books to squash you, or canes to whip you. In fact it was nothing more than a small cupboard, inside which there was nothing but complete darkness and total silence.

'At first you think it's no big deal,' said Neet, 'you think you can just sit it out and wait for the door to open. But you're wrong. First, the darkness starts to seep into your head. Then you start feeling dizzy and you can't tell whether you've been in there for two minutes or two whole hours. And then...' Neet paused for effect, 'you start to panic.'

'I wouldn't panic,' said Frankie, trying to sound brave.

'That's what you think,' said Neet, 'but nobody has ever been able to stand it. All your worst fears swim to the surface. If you're afraid of spiders, you start to see them crawling all over your face. If you're afraid of ghosts, you start to hear horrible wails. And there's no escape. Some people have never got over it.' Frankie took another glance at the table of grey-looking seniors, robotically eating their peas.

'We have to do *something*,' Frankie whispered.

'You do what you like,' said Neet, 'But I'm keeping a low profile. If I mess up this year, everyone will think I'm an idiot.'

'Just because you can't do *exams*,' said Frankie,

'doesn't mean you're an idiot.' But Neet was already face down in her lunch and snoring like a cement mixer.

As Frankie unpacked his belongings that evening, he thought about the old gentleman who had carried his trunk. 'Neet?' he asked, 'You know that old porter with the white hair?'

'Who, Goldie?' said Neet.

'Maybe. Why do you call him Goldie?' asked Frankie, puzzled.

'It's short for Goldfish,' Neet explained. 'He can't remember anything for more than five minutes. Like a goldfish going round and round in his bowl. Anyway, what about him?'

'Do you think he was a pupil here?' asked Frankie, 'Do you think that's why he's gone dotty?'

'Perhaps,' yawned Neet, 'but even if he was, he wouldn't remember. I'm off to bed. Goodnight

Frankie, see you in the morning.' Neet sauntered out of the boys' dormitory and headed towards the girls' quarters.

With Neet gone, Frankie felt restless. He wandered over to the small, barred window of the dormitory and gazed out into the courtyard. As a cloud pulled away from the moon, it illuminated a stone statue of a tall, thin man in a long robe. The statue was resting a foot on a pile of stone books and, on the tips of his fingers, he balanced what looked like a giant football. Frankie took a closer look. No. It wasn't a football. It was a globe and the stone man was staring at it as if he were about to lick his lips and take a huge bite. Squinting, Frankie could just make out the gold-plated inscription at the base of the statue: DR CALUS GORE, HEADMASTER.

CHAPTER NINE
DR CALUS GORE

The assembly hall was buzzing with nervous first years. 'What's going on?' yawned Frankie who hadn't slept a wink. He'd been kept up all night by a recording of the times-tables blaring through the dormitory speakers. According to Neet you were supposed to learn them in your sleep – if you could get to sleep that is.

'Dr Gore is on his way,' said Neet. 'He's going to give us our test results.'

A small boy sitting next to them pricked up his ears, 'Do you think there'll be prizes?' he asked. 'At my old school there were always prizes.'

'I doubt it,' said Neet. The boy looked disappointed.

'Are you a first year too?' asked Frankie, thinking the boy looked much too young to be at big school, 'I didn't see you in class.'

'That's because you're in 1D. I'm in 1A.'

'What's the difference?' said Frankie.

'It means he's a clever-clogs,' said Neet. The boy blushed with embarrassment, but also pride.

'My mum and dad thought my last school was too easy for me,' he sniffed. 'They sent me here to be stretched.'

'Ouch!' laughed Frankie. But the boy didn't see the joke.

'I'm very advanced for my age,' he said, 'I'm only six-and-a-half you know.'

'Six!' gasped Neet. 'Shouldn't you be in a sandpit or something?!' The boy looked cross.

'What's your name?' asked Frankie.

'Wesley Jones.'

'Can I call you Wes?' asked Neet.

'No,' said Wesley folding his arms, 'I like my name the way it is.' Neet looked at Frankie and rolled her eyes.

Suddenly, as if all the air had been sucked out of the room, everyone fell silent. Standing on stage, in long black robes, was Dr Calus Gore, as still as his stone statue. He had a huge bushy moustache and a bulging stare that reminded Frankie of one of those newts you're not supposed to squeeze in case their eyes pop out. But Frankie was not even tempted to laugh. There was something about Dr Gore that made his blood run cold. The headmaster squinted at the first years as if he were inspecting bacteria under a microscope. Then, sniffing loudly, he addressed his anxious audience.

'EX LUTO AURUM' he rasped in a voice that sounded like nails scraping down a blackboard. 'Do any of you know what it means? Indeed... do any of you know anything at all?' Wesley thrust his hand in the air.

'Is it a foreign language, Sir?'

'"Is it a foreign language, Sir?" How amusing,' Dr Gore sneered, 'Of course it's a foreign language. Even a gibbon would know it's a foreign language. The question is, what does it *meeeeean*?' Wesley sank back into his seat, crestfallen. 'EX LUTO AURUM,' Dr Gore repeated. 'From Mud, Gold. It is our school motto and my personal mission. Let's start with a bit of History, shall we?' Frankie was bored already. 'For centuries,' Gore continued, 'mankind has tried to turn mud into precious metals. But nobody has discovered the secret. Nobody, that is, except me!' He posed for a second as if expecting a round of applause.

'Neet is right,' muttered Frankie, 'He's off his nut.'

'I can hear your tiny brains whirring already,' the headmaster continued, 'How is such a thing possible? How can useless filth be turned into shining lumps of gold? Well, it's devilishly complicated, of course, but I shall make it simple for you.' Dr Gore breathed deeply through his pinched nostrils as if he really couldn't be bothered to explain.

'Every single one of you,' he smirked, 'is a grubby little dungball that your parents have, quite rightly, shovelled out of their fine homes. Your mums and dads are sick of you because, to put it simply, you are fools. Indeed, children are the most foolish creatures on the planet. Would anyone care to tell me why?' Nobody dared raise their hand. 'Right, then let me tell you. You stuff your skulls with stories and games and let's-pretend, squandering what little brainpower you have on pointless questions like, does the tooth-fairy exist? Well, I've got news for you – she doesn't'. A little boy at the back started to cry. 'But, you should count yourselves lucky,' the headmaster continued, 'because you are the mud, the slop, the raw sewage that I, Dr Calus Gore, shall transform into gold. By the time I've finished with you, you won't have time for dreams and ideas and stories. No!' Dr Gore stabbed the air with his finger, 'You will be twenty-four carat, top-of-the-range *exam*-passing machines!'

As soon as he had uttered the word, a loud, gurgling sound echoed round the room. The headmaster's eyes went completely round as if somebody had stuck a pin in his bottom. 'Who...' he hissed violently, 'is snoring?' Frankie glanced across at Neet and sure enough, she was fast asleep and whistling through her nose. Dr Gore strode towards her, his eyes practically popping out of his head. Then, without taking his eyes off the unlucky girl, he reached into his gown and pulled out a fat white rat. The rat squealed and wriggled as Dr Gore dangled it by its tail.

'What is that?!' Frankie gasped under his breath.

'That's Snuffles,' whispered Wesley anxiously, 'The headmaster's pet.' Dr Gore stepped towards the sleeping Neet and, pulling her collar to one side, dropped the rat down the back of her school blazer. Neet woke with a lurch.

'*Woooooooooh*!' she yelled as the rat scampered all over her, 'Get it off me! Get it off me!' The first years watched in horror as Neet clutched and tugged at her new school uniform.

'Stop it!' shouted Frankie, leaping to his feet. But the headmaster's yellow eyes were glowing with amusement. Frankie lunged forward, seized

Snuffles's tail and pulled him out of Neet's sleeve. The rat squealed and bit Frankie savagely on the hand, before scampering up on to his master's shoulder.

'Good boy, Snuffles,' cooed Dr Gore, feeding it a biscuit. To Frankie's disgust, the greedy rodent seized it between its paws and chainsawed through it with its massive incisors. Dr Gore turned his head slowly towards them. 'Names?' he hissed between strange triangular teeth.

'Anita Banerjee,' squeaked Neet, unable to look the headmaster in the eye.

'Well, well, well,' sneered Dr Gore, 'Another Banerjee. How tedious. You?'

'Frankie Blewitt,' mumbled Frankie, licking the wound on his hand. Dr Gore eyeballed him suspiciously.

'I should have known,' he sneered. 'Your father's told me all about you.' Then, shoving

Frankie back in his seat, he hauled Neet up on to the stage. 'So, Miss Banerjee,' he said, circling her like a shark, 'Know it all already do you? Think you can take a nice little nap when I'm speaking do you?'

'No, no!' said Neet, 'it's not like that...'

'Judging by your execrable performance in yesterday's test, I dare say you don't have so much as a mung bean between those silly little ears of yours. But don't worry...' Dr Gore's lips stretched into a piranha smile, 'I'm giving you a second chance.'

'Oh. Thank you, Sir' said Neet uncertainly.

'Now, Anita,' continued Dr Gore, resting a hand on Neet's shoulder, 'perhaps you could tell the class the answer to the first question. What is the capital of Chile?'

'Um. I don't know that one Sir,' said Neet.

'Well not knowing is not good enough is it,

Anita? Luckily I have something to focus your mind.' Dr Gore reached into the folds of his gown and whipped out a small red bottle. 'Extra-Spicy Chilli Sauce,' he declared, holding up the bottle for the class to see, 'direct from the fair nation of Chile. Open wide, Banerjee.' Neet did as she was told and the headmaster dripped some of the burning hot sauce onto Neet's tongue.

'Ahhhhh! Ah! Ah!' Neet gripped her throat, turning redder and redder as the fiery liquid began to sting.

'Keep thinking, Banerjee!' sneered Gore. 'Or it's more of the chilli sauce.'

'Um... Paris? Um, um, America? Um...' Neet was guessing wildly.

'Stop it!' shouted Frankie, 'It's not fair!'

'QUIET, BLEWITT.' bellowed Gore, tipping more sauce down Neet's throat.

Then, just when Frankie thought that his

friend would burst into a ball of flames, Neet's face screwed up in concentration.

'Saggy-Aunty?' she said. Dr Gore peered at her closely, 'Pants-a-gogo?' Neet stared straight ahead of her, searching for the right answer.

'What rubbish!' scoffed Dr Gore. But Frankie could see the headmaster was puzzled. Neet was homing in on something.

'Santa-Clueso, Anty-aga.' Frankie couldn't work out how Neet was doing it. Then, out of the corner of his eye, he saw something moving. It was Wesley! He knew the answer and was mouthing it silently to Neet. 'San—ti—a—go?' Neet ventured. Wesley nodded, 'Santiago! SANTIAGO!' shouted Neet deliriously.

Dr Gore was so furious you could have fried an egg on his head. 'Cheat!' he screeched. 'Somebody told you the answer didn't they?' Dr Gore's yellow gaze flashed rapidly about the room as if he were surrounded by snipers. 'Don't think you can trick me!' he shrieked, pointing wildly about him, 'I can smell conspiracy a mile off!' Wesley turned white and bit his lip. 'I'd say it was you, Frankie Blewitt,' Gore yelled, foaming at the mouth, 'if you weren't so notoriously dim-witted.' Then, levelling himself with the terrified Neet, he fixed her with his bulgy eyes, 'Which of your sinister little accomplices...' he hissed. But Neet was hardly listening. All that chilli sauce had made her feel a little bit ill – a little bit windy, to be precise. Without warning Neet burped up a huge fiery belch, setting fire to the headmaster's carefully trimmed moustache. 'AwoooooOOOO!' he shrieked, leaping around the assembly hall like a demonic rabbit, 'Water! Water!' Dr Gore was in such utter panic, he grabbed the nearest fire extinguisher and drenched himself from head to foot. The water hissed and spluttered as the first years dissolved into fits of giggles.

'So much for keeping a low profile,' Frankie chuckled, 'Nice one Neet!' Neet blushed with pride.

'Thanks for helping me out, Wes,' she said, turning to Wesley. 'You're a life-saver!'

'Shhhh! You'll get me in trouble!' Wes whispered, 'And it's Wes-LEY!'

Then, as if a cloud had passed in front of the sun, the room suddenly darkened. Dr Gore was towering over them, steam rising from his unusually large forehead. He glared at the first years one by one as if he could see right through to their bones.

'I see we have some rogue elements,' he hissed like a boiling kettle. 'Some free electrons, some rebel spirits. But let me make one thing clear,' he fixed Frankie with his burning eyes, 'Very soon, all *resistance* will be useless!' Then, with a twitch of his frazzled moustache, the headmaster swept out of the hall like a sinister black flag.

CHAPTER TEN
PEAS AND PUDDING

Frankie's first week at Crammar Grammar was a series of tests, homework and bowls of oily peas. The first years were moved so quickly from one classroom to the next that they hardly had time to breathe, let alone think. But there was one question that was on Frankie's mind all week. 'What do you reckon Dr Gore meant,' he asked Neet while they were sitting in the common room before Sunday morning classes, 'when he said that soon all resistance will be useless?'

'Dunno,' grumbled Neet who was trying to

snooze on a hard bench, 'I don't understand a word he says.' Frankie cracked his knuckles in thought. The whole school gave him the creeps. It was like Neet said; he felt like a lab-rat in a huge experiment. But he had the creeping suspicion that there was worse to come, much worse.

'He must have meant something. *Very soon*, he said... Neet?' Neet opened one eye.

'What do you want?'

'I think it's time to give it a try.'

'Try what? What are you talking about Frankie?'

'Resistance! Listen, we've been here for a week and all we've done is learn lists, take tests and eat peas. It's doing my head in.'

'It's meant to,' she yawned.

'Well I'm fed up with it. It's time for a change.'

'What do you mean?' said Neet.

'Come with me and I'll tell you.' Frankie threw

on his jacket and headed for the door, 'We're going to find Goldie.'

Goldie lived in the games shed. Now, as you know, most games sheds are full of footballs and hurdles and skipping ropes, but, because there were never any games at Crammar Grammar, Goldie had turned it into a tiny but comfortable home. Well, actually, it was more like a nest. The inside walls of the shed were lined with scraps of paper reminding Goldie to do things he might otherwise forget, but because the shed was so very small they had started to creep over the ceiling as well. In fact, Goldie's shed was so minuscule there wasn't even room for a bed. So, instead, the porter slept upright in his chair with a blanket over his knees. But Goldie never grumbled. It was bad manners to grumble and Goldie's manners were impeccable. So long as there was tea in the pot and a jug of milk on the table, he thought himself lucky enough.

'Slow down, Frankie,' yelled Neet, as they approached the games shed, 'What's the hurry?'

'We need to get the keys to Dr Gore's study,' Frankie explained, 'before lessons start.'

Neet screeched to a halt. 'Are you kidding? I'm not breaking into Gore's study! I'm keeping a low profile, remember?!'

'I think you blew that when you set fire to Dr Gore's moustache!' joked Frankie.

'Hmmm, I don't know,' said Neet, 'What if our parents find out?' Frankie shuddered. He'd been trying not to think about that.

'Resistance is not easy-peasy-pip-squeak,' he said, trying to remember what Alphonsine had told him, but Neet just looked confused. 'I mean, we have to do *something*,' continued Frankie, 'or it'll be oily peas and tests forever and we'll end up turning into giant calculators!' Neet sighed.

'Okay, but how do we get the keys? Goldie isn't just going to hand them over is he?'

'Oh...' In his eagerness Frankie hadn't really thought through all the details of his plan. But luckily, Neet had a bright idea.

'If you distract him,' she said, 'then I could sneak inside and pin a note on the wall and...' she glanced around furtively to check whether there were any prefects lurking nearby and, just to be safe, she leaned in and whispered the rest.

'That's brilliant, Neet!' cried Frankie. 'You're a genius!' Neet grinned from ear to ear.

'Well then, let's go!'

There was only one thing that interested Goldie as much as a freshly brewed cup of tea and that was a beautiful butterfly. Goldie adored butterflies and had grown a huge rambling rosebush over his shed that attracted the creatures in all colours and varieties. There were delicate white ones, dashing red ones, and dazzling blue ones that looked like they'd been peeled off the sky. As Neet and Frankie made their way to the games shed, Goldie was sitting outside admiring a large orange-and-black specimen that had just settled on a rosebud.

'Hello, you two,' he smiled, 'Come and look at this splendid fellow. Isn't he marvellous?' Frankie went to inspect while Neet slipped round the back, silent as an eel.

'It's lovely,' said Frankie, and it really was. The butterfly opened its wings to display two magnificent blue circles.

'Those are false eyes,' Goldie explained. 'They trick birds into thinking that the butterfly is a much larger animal, like a cat or a fox. It scares them away. Clever, eh?' The butterfly beat its wings and settled on Goldie's outstretched finger, 'You may not believe it, but some butterflies are even more marvellous than this one. Once, I saw the loveliest butterfly in the world. I'd never seen one like it before and I've never seen one since.'

'What did it look like?' Frankie asked as the weightless creature tumbled away on the breeze. Goldie blinked his eyes and looked up at the sky.

'I can't remember,' he said, 'I just know it was the loveliest butterfly in the world.'

Neet popped out from behind the shed and gave Frankie the thumbs up. So far, so good.

'Goldie,' Frankie said nicely, 'could you give us the keys to Dr Gore's study please?' Goldie looked puzzled.

'Um... um... I don't think I can do that I'm afraid. Not without a note from Dr Gore.' Frankie felt a bit rotten for tricking him, but there were bigger fish to fry.

'But you *have* a note,' Frankie insisted, 'He told us he sent you one this morning.'

'Oh? Well, um… let me check.' Goldie put on his spectacles and went inside to inspect. His eye immediately settled on a note that said in big writing: REMEMBER TO GIVE KEYS TO FRANKIE BLEWITT AND ANITA BANERJEE. Goldie scratched his head in confusion. 'This is most irregular,' he paused and looked at Frankie over his glasses, 'May I ask what business you have in Dr Gore's study?' Frankie racked his brains for something to say as Goldie's eyebrows began to lift with suspicion, 'I must say, I can't think of any possible reason why Dr Gore would…'

'Punishment!' exclaimed Neet suddenly.

'Yes! That's right,' said Frankie, picking up the thread, 'We're being punished. We have to put all of Dr Gore's books in reverse alphabetical order. Don't we Neet?' Neet nodded and Goldie frowned gravely.

'Deary-me,' he tutted. Frankie and Neet glanced at each other nervously. 'Well if it's as bad as that,' he continued, 'I suppose you had better get started.' Then, with a quiet chuckle, he unhooked a small bunch of keys from his belt and handed them over.

'Mission accomplished!' Frankie and Neet shouted as they raced across the deserted playing fields and up the stony steps to the headmaster's study.

As the door closed behind them, the two friends felt as if they'd been trapped in a giant coffin. Dr Gore's study was heavy with polished wood and a thick smell of mothballs hung on the velvet curtains. Everything about it, from the monstrous bookshelves to the throne-like armchair, was designed to make the headmaster look extremely important.

'Wowee,' Neet couldn't help murmuring as she gazed at the high walls covered from top to bottom with framed portraits of Dr Gore winning prizes and shaking famous hands. But pride of place went to a procession of framed certificates hanging behind the headmasterly desk.

'Look at them!' said Frankie, gawping in awe.

'Told you he was clever,' said Neet, anxiously glancing over her shoulder. But Frankie's eye had been drawn to one particularly extravagant frame.

'That's strange,' he said, 'This prize doesn't belong to the headmaster. It was won by somebody called Lucas Rego.'

'The Bowbell Prize for Science,' read Neet, 'Isn't that the most important prize in the world?'

'I think you're right,' said Frankie. 'What's it doing in Gore's office?' But Neet wasn't really listening. All those portraits of the headmaster were making her twitchy.

'Let's get on with it, Frankie,' she whispered.

Frankie climbed into Gore's enormous leather armchair, picked up the phone and dialled the school kitchens. Mrs Piggot, the dinner lady, answered.

'Dr Gore?' she wheezed, 'My, my, you're up early. What can I do for you?' Frankie held his nose to disguise his voice.

'There's been a change to the school menu,' he said in the most headmasterly voice he could muster. There was a pause at the other end of the line.

'Are you alright there, Sir? You sound a bit off colour.'

'I am a bit off colour,' Frankie continued, giving a little cough for good measure. 'I'd like a nice large helping of your very best peas in fish oil to put me right.'

'Are you sure about that, Sir?' said Mrs Piggot,

'It's filthy stuff you know, I wouldn't give it to worms. Children are the only thing it's good for – you said so yourself.'

'All the same,' Frankie continued, 'a nice large helping of peas for me please. And sausages and mashed potatoes for the pupils.' Mrs Piggott could hardly believe her ears. But she didn't dare argue with the headmaster.

'Very well then, Sir. Is that all?'

Neet tugged Frankie's sleeve, 'and pudding!' she whispered.

'And pudding.'

'You *are* a bit off colour aren't you, Sir? Perhaps you should go back to bed.'

'No, no. Nothing a bowl of peas can't fix.'

'If you say so, Sir,' snorted Mrs Piggot, and hung up.

When the girls and boys of Crammar Grammar

went to lunch later that day they could hardly believe their luck. The dining hall was usually silent except for the slow scraping of forks, but that afternoon it was gurgling with laughter. Rather than ladling out oily peas, the dinner ladies were serving up bangers and mash, and for pudding there was apple crumble and custard. So many people were going back for seconds that Mrs Piggot was wheezing like a punctured beachball. For just one hour, the school was utterly transformed. Even Wesley, who usually forced down every pea on his plate, was thrilled with the change of menu.

But one person was not thrilled. One person was not thrilled at all. Dr Gore marched into the dining hall holding his plate at arm's length.

'What is *this*?' he sniffed, shoving his plate under Mrs Piggot's nose.

'Peas, Sir?' explained Mrs Piggot, 'in fish oil.'

Dr Gore rolled his eyes.

'I can see that they're *peeeeeas*. The question is, what are they doing on my plate?'

'It's w-w-what you asked for, isn't it, Sir?' stammered Mrs Piggot, beginning to realise something was wrong. Dr Gore sighed impatiently.

'Of course it isn't what I asked for, you dippy old trout. Now where are my sausages?' Mrs Piggot turned red as a radish.

'The s-s-sausages are g-g-gone, Sir. The ch-ch-children ate them.'

'WHAT?' Dr Gore flashed his eyes round the hall. Sure enough, every child in the dining room was shovelling down their sausages as fast as they possibly could.

'Who is responsible for this ATROCITY!?' screeched the headmaster stalking round the room like an angry ostrich. Everybody focused on their plates and tried to avoid Dr Gore's yellow gaze. Everybody, that is, except Frankie. He was laughing so hard, the tears were rolling down his face. He stuffed a sausage into his mouth to try and stifle his giggles, but it was too late. The headmaster was already striding over to his table. Seizing Frankie by the back of his blazer, Dr Gore lifted him level with his newt-like stare. 'I think it's time for a little chat, don't you?' he hissed through his pointed teeth. Then, with Frankie thrashing about like a fish on a line, Dr Gore marched up to his study.

CHAPTER ELEVEN
THE HOLE

Frankie's heart was beating so quickly, he thought it would explode. He stood alone, at the centre of the study, while Dr Gore tapped his rickety fingers on the desk.

'Many children have come to this school,' he sniffed, squinting at Frankie as if he were something he'd just pulled out of his nose, 'all of them poisonous little toads. But every now and then a particularly noxious specimen arrives who threatens to pollute the minds of the others. Do you understand what I'm saying, Blewitt?'

Frankie nodded. 'You're saying I'm a noxious specimen, Sir.'

'Very good! Give the boy a prize!' Dr Gore curled his lips into a sarcastic grimace. 'But what you fail to understand is that I have ways of – how can I put it? – I have ways of neutralising toxic creatures like yourself.'

Frankie wasn't sure what *neutralise* meant, but he didn't like the sound of it. 'But, I don't want to be neutralised!' he panicked.

'Did you hear that, Snuffles?' Dr Gore called to his rat, 'Frankie Blewitt doesn't want to be neutralised.' Snuffles snickered through a mouthful of biscuit, and rubbed his greasy little paws. 'Do you think your parents sent you here to do what *you* want? Do you think they sent you here to play football and dream up stories and eat my sausages?' Dr Gore's eyes flashed a strange acid colour and Frankie began to feel his face burn. 'No, is the answer you're looking for. When you are at Crammar Grammar you do not do what *you* want, you do what *I* want.' Frankie didn't reply. 'You can begin by telling me the names of your collaborators.'

'What do you mean?' said Frankie.

'Oh, come on, Blewitt, don't try to be clever. I want the names of your co-conspirators, your henchmen, the other gang members who helped you pull off this sordid little trick. I bet that Anita Banerjee was involved. She's a crafty little weasel.'

'No she isn't!' Frankie protested, 'She's my friend!'

'Exactly. An accomplice.'

'No!' cried Frankie. 'Neet had nothing to do with it. It was all my idea. I did it on my own.'

'How very noble,' hissed Dr Gore. 'Not only a terrorist, but an accomplished liar.'

The headmaster opened a drawer in his desk and produced a bottle of green capsules. Frankie gasped as he caught sight of the label. *Telitol*. Those were the tablets that Alphonsine had told him about. The ones that made you blab the truth whether you liked it or not. Dr Gore pinched Frankie's nose, shoved the capsule between his teeth and clamped his lips shut. Frankie couldn't breathe. He wriggled like a gerbil until he thought he'd suffocate. Then, just as the pill began to slip to the back of his throat, he remembered the trick Alphonsine had taught him. Frankie curled his tongue around the capsule, shoved it up between his gum and his cheek and pretended to gulp it down.

'That's more like it,' said Dr Gore, releasing Frankie's nose. 'Now let's try again shall we? What are the names of your fellow conspirators?'

Taking care not to dislodge the capsule,

Frankie slowly replied, 'Nobody, Sir.' Dr Gore's moustache twitched with irritation. He peered at Frankie a little closer.

'Are you absolutely sure?'

'Yes, Sir.' Dr Gore didn't trust Frankie, but he did trust the tablet. After all, he had improved the formula himself.

'Well, well, well,' he muttered, putting down his pen, 'what a disappointment you are.' The headmaster sighed, 'Do you know what your father told me?' Frankie shook his head. 'He said that having a son was like having an insect land on the end of your nose. Extremely irritating, but impossible to swat.' Frankie felt angry tears sting his eyes, but he managed to blink them away.

'Well. If, as you say, you acted alone, I will simply have to double your punishment.' The headmaster strode over to the wall displaying his certificates and, to Frankie's curiosity, stopped at the Bowbell prize – the one that didn't belong to him. Dr Gore lifted the frame and unhooked a key hanging behind it. Then, with a flick of his wrist, he opened a small door hidden in the panelled office wall. Inside was nothing but blackness.

'The trouble with children like you, Blewitt,' the headmaster said wearily, 'is that you are too stupid to be afraid. Thankfully, there is nothing a few hours in the Hole can't fix.' Before Frankie had the chance to run, Dr Gore seized him by the collar, shoved him into the tiny cupboard and locked the door.

It was so dark inside the Hole that Frankie couldn't tell if his eyes were open or closed and it was so silent that he could hear nothing but his heartbeat. He spat out the Telitol tablet and slipped it into his blazer pocket. Then, crouching down in the narrow space, he rested his forehead against his knees.

'Nothing to be afraid of,' he told himself, 'I'll just sit here and wait. No problem.' But the darkness and the silence were so intense that he could already feel icy drops of sweat slithering down his spine. 'Nothing to be afraid of,' he repeated in a whisper. But he could hear the tremors in his voice. The darkness began to warp and flex, so that Frankie could no longer tell if he was locked in a tiny box or floating in outer space. He tried screwing up his eyes and plugging his ears, but it only made things worse. The darkness seemed to be seeping through his skin, right into the centre of his bones. Then, just as Neet had described, he was gripped by the most electrifying nightmares.

Looming over him, his fist clenching a rolled -up newspaper, was none other than his father.

Frankie yelped. Mr Blewitt was twenty times his normal size and was thwacking the paper against the palm of his hand, 'WHAT DID I TELL YOU FRANKIE?' bellowed the vision, 'FAILURE IS NOT AN OPTION.'

'Sorry, Dad! I'm sorry!' squeaked Frankie in fright. Then, as if in a dream, he saw himself as a grubby little fly buzzing helplessly in circles. Mr Blewitt swiped at him with his newspaper while Frankie dodged and dived, beating his flimsy wings, 'Stop it, Dad!' he buzzed, 'I'm sorry.'

'"F" is for FAILURE!' shouted Mr Blewitt, waving his paper in the air, '"F" is for FRANKIE!' Frankie howled and pressed his eyes to his knees. '"F" for FAILURE. "F" for FRANKIE.' Frankie heard a terrible ringing in his ears.

Then, all of a sudden, without warning, another voice whispered through the darkness. It was a French voice. And it said just three words. I bet you can guess what they were…

PANTS ON HEAD

Frankie swallowed hard and looked up at his dad who was snorting and puffing like an angry walrus. Then he closed his eyes tight and imagined the silliest pair of underpants he could possibly think of.

'What the blazes?!' Frankie opened one eye and saw that Mr Blewitt had a lovely big pair of spotty underpants, wedged right down over his eyes. 'What the devil is going on?' he shouted, tugging at the elastic. But they wouldn't budge. Frankie felt a surge of laughter welling up in his belly, 'I suppose you think this is funny?' yelled Mr Blewitt, swiping the air blindly with his newspaper. 'You just wait till I—' Suddenly, Mr Blewitt's arm halted in mid-air. It looked like the newspaper had ideas of its own. It wriggled out of

Mr Blewitt's grasp, twisted itself around and delivered a solid blow to his backside.

'OUCH!' squawked Mr Blewitt, 'That hurt!' *THWACK*! The newspaper struck again. *THWACK! THWACK! THWACK!* 'Ouch! Ouch! Ouch!' squealed Mr Blewitt, 'Oweeee!' And, as quickly as it had come, the nightmare disappeared into the darkness, running and howling and clutching its sore behind.

Frankie lay slumped on the floor of the cupboard – out of breath but completely calm. 'Just nightmares,' Frankie told himself, 'nothing to be afraid of.' And Frankie wasn't afraid any more. The Hole was just a dark little broom cupboard. A bit quiet and a bit smelly, and that was all. He sat up straight and ran his fingers over the walls, searching for a way out. The door that opened on to Gore's study was jammed shut, but as Frankie felt the back of the cupboard, his fingers came across a second keyhole. *That's strange,* thought Frankie, *There's another door.* He pushed against it with his feet but it was locked tight. *Hmmm.* Frankie shoved his hands in his pockets as he wondered what to do next and, as he did so, his fingers scrunched up against a bunch of keys. Of course! He still had the spare keys to Gore's office. He ran his fingertips over them in the darkness. There were four or five different keys on the ring. One of them had to work. He tried them out one by one and, sure enough, the final key turned as easily as a fish in water. 'What's he hiding in here?' Frankie muttered to himself as he pushed the door open, but it was so dark, he couldn't even see his hands in front of his face. Then, all of a sudden, there was a pulse of dim, purplish light that seemed to come from below. Frankie took a sharp breath and looked around. He was standing at the top of a dizzyingly steep stone staircase and at the bottom, round the corner, something was hissing and purring. Frankie steadied himself against the walls, his heart pounding against his ribcage. He had to know what was down there. But just as he was about to take a step, he heard a key jostle in the outside lock.

Having enjoyed listening to Frankie yell and howl for a good hour or so, the headmaster was puzzled to hear his captive go quiet and had come to investigate. Frankie couldn't risk being caught. He quickly locked himself back in the cupboard and, just as he was stuffing the keys back into his pocket, the dusty light of the study pricked his eyes.

'Any more of your funny business and I'll lock you in there for the rest of the term,' hissed the headmaster, dragging Frankie out of the Hole. 'Now I don't want to see your grubby little face in here again. Understood?'

'Of course, Dr Gore.' Frankie replied as politely as he could. But nothing could have been further from the truth.

CHAPTER TWELVE
ALL OF US

Neet was stuck in a triple Latin class with Mr Lupi – a decrepit old goblin who was probably around when the Romans were throwing people to the lions. As usual, Mr Lupi was perched in his chair squawking like an ancient parrot, but Neet was too worried to concentrate.

'Where is Frankie? What has Dr Gore done to him?' she frowned and fretted, chewing on the end of her pen.

At long last Frankie entered the classroom and slipped into his seat. 'Frankie!' Neet smiled a big inky smile, 'Are you okay?'

'Yes, I'm fine, but we've got to go back to Gore's study as soon as we can.'

'Why? What for?' Mr Lupi's ears were beginning to twitch suspiciously, so Frankie scribbled her a note explaining all about the Hole and the secret door and the gloomy staircase.

'He's keeping something down there,' whispered Frankie. 'I think it's his Big Discovery.'

'What makes you say that?' said Neet.

'On my first day here Goldie said something to me about Dr Gore having big plans for this place. Then, the other day, Dr Gore himself told us that soon resistance would be useless. I think something is about to happen Neet, and whatever it is, it's at the bottom of those stairs.'

Over the next few days, Frankie and Neet kept a

careful eye on Dr Gore's movements, waiting for the opportunity to break back into his study. But the headmaster hardly left his office at all. Frankie and Neet were just beginning to wonder if they would ever find a way back in, when a notice appeared on the school board:

Volunteers required.
Assemble in hall after classes on Thursday.
Dr Gore.

'Great,' said Frankie, 'he'll be out of his office for at least half an hour. This is our best chance.' So, on Thursday afternoon, as the other first years trooped dutifully into the hall, Neet and Frankie gave everyone the slip and snuck back into the headmaster's study.

Frankie unlocked the hidden door with Goldie's keys, then crept through the Hole and opened the second door that led to the steep stone stairs. Frankie went first, feeling his way down the walls with Neet following closely behind. It was so dark, and the stairs so slippery, that they had to tread very carefully and very slowly.

'I don't like this Frankie!' grumbled Neet as they turned the corner, 'I don't like this at all. What if there's a...' Suddenly there was a dim throb of light and, deep in the darkness, Frankie and Neet saw the flash of fangs. 'MONSTER!' Neet yelled, scrambling back up the stairs, 'MOOOOOOONSTER!' Frankie caught her round the ankles.

'Wait Neet! Stop!' cried Frankie, who had seen more clearly through the gloom. Frankie patted the walls to find the light switch and, as the electric bulb flickered on, they saw that they were standing in the middle of a vast, churning laboratory.

The laboratory was crammed with bottles and test-tubes, hissing and dripping and bubbling with sinister fluids, and perched on a shelf alongside some other dismal-looking creatures, was a poor stuffed monkey.

'That's your monster Neet,' said Frankie, pointing up at the stiff little animal snarling helplessly down at them. Neet picked herself up and went to inspect. Alongside the monkey were turtles in bottles, dissected frogs and dead butterflies pinned to a board in a tidy pattern.

'Goldie would go mad,' she murmured as she gazed at the neat little massacre. But Frankie was already sorting through the dozens of bottles that crowded the workbench.

'Look Neet, Telitol tablets. Gore tried to give me one of these. And get a load of this: Brain-Aid... Milk of Amnesia...' Frankie took a sniff and almost choked. It stank of mouldy cheese.

'Smell that,' he said, holding the bottle under Neet's nose.

'Urgh! Thanks a lot Frankie!' she spluttered. Frankie stoppered the bottle and put it back on the bench.

'I can't believe he's been trying out this stuff on everyone at school. He really is crazy.'

Suddenly, a weird purple glow shuddered in the glass of the   bottles. They looked behind them and blinked into the strange light. Before them was a savage-looking steel machine bristling with tubes and wires. The light was radiating from a tank connected to the device by a tangle of pipes and filled with a dark violet gas that pulsed and glowed like an angry bruise. Frankie felt as if he were in the presence of a dangerous beast.

I think this is it,' he whispered. They crept

towards it, as if they were afraid of waking it up. At the centre of the contraption was a child-sized chair and, hovering above it, was an odd little helmet. Frankie walked around the machine. The tank of gas was linked to the helmet by a plastic pipe that ended just where the right ear would be, and on the left side was another pipe, like the one you'd find on a vacuum cleaner, leading to a large test tube.

'It's a time machine,' said Neet, 'I saw one like

it in a movie.'

'Really?' said Frankie, 'But why would Dr Gore want a time machine?' As he moved around the grim device, Frankie stumbled into a box and knocked it open with a crash.

Neet jumped like a startled cat.

'Careful, Frankie!' she hushed, 'Dr Gore will know someone's been here!' But Frankie was already inspecting the contents of the box. Inside were dozens of glass test tubes, just like the one screwed into the machine, and glued onto every tube was a small label.

Frankie picked one up. 'Jack Elderton,' he read. 'Isn't he in the other first year class?' Frankie picked up another, 'Maximus Platten. He sits next to me for triple Maths.' Frankie rummaged through the box, 'Elise and Marcus Overd, Theo Lonsdale, Anna and Colin O'Brien...' Frankie stared at Neet in horror. 'We're all here! There's a test-tube for everyone! Whatever Dr Gore is doing, he's going to do it to all of us!'

CHAPTER THIRTEEN
THE BRAIN-DRAIN MACHINE

A key turned in the door at the top of the stairs. Frankie dived for the light switch and the pair quickly hid themselves behind the box of test-tubes. 'I thought we had more time!' squeaked Neet. Frankie and Neet hardly dared breathe as footsteps began to tap down the stairs. But there was not just one pair of footsteps. There were two. Dr Gore's voice scraped down the passageway.

'This is a real privilege,' he slithered. 'A prize, if you like. Only the very cleverest pupils are allowed to help me with my experiments.'

'Thank you, Dr Gore,' a small voice rang out. 'I won't disappoint you, I promise.' Neet and Frankie gasped. It was Wesley.

'Now, I do believe,' said Dr Gore, barely suppressing his excitement, 'that my invention is almost perfect. All you need to do is to give it a little test drive.' Wesley hesitated at the sight of the machine, which had begun to growl like an angry dog.

'What does it do?' he asked.

'Now, now,' said the headmaster, becoming impatient, 'clever children don't ask questions. Clever children do as they're told.'

'But...' Wesley began.

'But what?' snapped the headmaster, 'Do you want to be head boy one day or don't you?'

'Yes! Yes I do, but...'

'Marvellous,' said Dr Gore smoothly. 'Now there's nothing to worry about, just make yourself comfortable in this chair.'

'We have to warn him Frankie!' whispered Neet. They peeked round the edge of the box and signalled silently to Wesley who looked startled, and rather cross to see them there. Neet put her finger to her lips and shook her head.

'Don't do it Wes!' she mouthed silently. But Wesley frowned in annoyance. This was his big chance to impress the headmaster and he wasn't about to let anybody mess it up.

'Wes – LEY,' he mouthed back, then looked away.

'In you get, Master Jones,' grinned Dr Gore.

Wesley took a breath, then slowly stepped into the machine and sat down. The moment he touched the seat, the helmet dropped and fastened itself tightly to his head.

'No need to worry, Master Jones,' said the headmaster, rubbing his hands together and

standing at a distance. 'Just make yourself nice and comfy.' The machine started to shake and tremble.

'Ooooooooh!' said Wesley, feeling more anxious by the second, 'I think I've changed my mind!'

But it was too late. Dr Gore was cranking up the power and grinning like a corpse. 'That's where you're wrong Master Jones!' he cackled as the machine set up a loud sucking noise 'It is *I* who am changing your mind!'

Wesley suddenly went completely silent and began to pull the most awful faces, as if he were chewing on an enormous gobstopper. Peeking round the edge of the box, Frankie saw the large test tube that was attached to the machine begin to fill with a fine, powdery gas that sparkled like crushed diamonds. 'That's the way!' shouted Dr Gore, 'Suck all that rubbish out of his silly little head. Ha ha!'

'What is he doing to Wesley?' whispered Frankie, 'It's awful!'

'I know,' said Neet, 'we have to stop him! Where's the plug?'

The two friends crawled around behind the boxes, searching desperately for the plug, but before they could find it the machine changed gear. Now that the test tube was full, instead of sucking, it began to pump the dark, purple gas out of the tank and into Wesley's right ear. Suddenly Frankie spotted the plug behind a workbench - he pulled it as quickly as he could, but it was too late. Wesley's face had gone completely still, and he was staring in front of him like a zombie.

'I truly am a genius!' hissed the headmaster as he lifted the dreadful helmet from Wesley's head. Wesley blinked blankly. 'A little question for you,' said Dr Gore, practically melting with excitement. 'What is the square root of 762,868, divided by 67 and multiplied by 152?'

Without even blinking Wesley murmured, '1,981.4972.' His voice was dull and robotic like those voices you hear in a lift, or at a train station. Wesley wasn't Wesley any more. Dr Gore's machine had turned him into a human computer!

'Clever boy!' crowed Dr Gore. 'Practically as clever as me, wouldn't you say?'

'Yes, Dr Gore.'

'You know why that is, Wesley?' continued the headmaster, tapping excitedly on the tank, 'I've filled your head with a colossal dose of brainpower, direct from my own skull.' Frankie and Neet stared at each other in horror. 'It took me months to build up the stock,' Dr Gore continued, swatting Snuffles who was clambering all over the machine and poking his nose into the tubes, 'but now I have enough for all your little friends. Two hundred litres of pure, concentrated genius!'

Poor Wesley didn't move a muscle. He just stared straight ahead of him like a dummy in a shop window. Dr Gore grabbed a phone from under a pile of papers and hastily dialled a number.

'Who is he calling?' whispered Neet.

'I don't know,' said Frankie 'but we'll have to find out.'

The headmaster paced up and down excitedly.

'I've cracked it!' he gabbled into the receiver, 'The Mind-Enhancer works a treat! I worked out how to...' The person on the other end cut him off short. 'Of course, Sir,' slithered Dr Gore, 'of course you don't give a rat's whisker about the details. How silly of me... Yes, everything's ready for the launch on Friday,' he chattered as if he were arranging a birthday party. 'I've invited the Minister for Education, the press, all the top brains and dignitaries. Ha ha! The other headmasters will choke with envy!' There was a buzzing from the other end of the line, 'No need to worry, Sir, that's all been taken care of. I have selected a particularly dim pupil for the demonstration. Indeed, this child is so preposterously dense that she can't even hear the word EXAM without passing out! Can you believe it?' Frankie felt his stomach clench.

'Neet!' he whispered, but Neet's head had already dropped on to her chest and, before Frankie had the chance to wake her she started snoring like a tractor. 'Wake up! Wake up!' whispered Frankie, shaking his friend urgently. But it was too late. Snuffles had pricked up his little pink ears and was scuttling in their direction.

'Eeeee! Eeeeeeeeeeeeeeee!' squeaked the rat at the top of his tiny voice. Neet woke with a jolt and Frankie slapped a hand over her mouth to stop her yelling.

'What's the matter, my pet?' cooed Dr Gore, stalking towards Frankie and Neet's hiding place.

'After three we run for it!' whispered Frankie, 'One, two...' Frankie and Neet leapt to their feet and tipped over the box, spilling test-tubes all over the floor.

'What? Blewitt! Banerjee! What are you doing here?' Dr Gore lunged out to snatch them but slipped on the tubes and tumbled backwards.

'Ruuuuuuuuuun!' yelled Frankie. With Gore snatching at their ankles, Frankie and Neet charged out of the laboratory and up the stairs. They ran as fast as they could, out of the headmaster's office, out of the building and across the school grounds. As they legged it towards the gates, Frankie felt a small, cold object bouncing against his chest. It was the dog whistle that Alphonsine had slipped round his neck the morning he left home. The gates were locked, but they managed to squeeze through the small gap between the railings and out onto the road. Frankie put the whistle to his lips and blew and blew and blew.

CHAPTER FOURTEEN
THE HIDEOUT

Neet and Frankie took cover in a ditch by the side of the road. The light was beginning to fade and the cold air bit their ears.

'Poor Wes,' whispered Neet. 'How are we going to get his brain back?'

'I don't know,' said Frankie, 'But I do know someone who can help us'.

There was a soft rumble in the distance, like the growl of a hungry belly. Frankie jumped to his feet and ran to the side of the road. 'Alphonsine!' Alphonsine's motorbike pounced

into view like a huge black puma.

'Wow! Who's that?' cried Neet.

'Hello, my friends!' shouted Alphonsine as her bike shuddered to a halt, 'Colette hear ze whistle and I come as quick as I can.' Colette yelped proudly and Alphonsine ruffled her fur, 'Look, I am still in my slippers.' Frankie dashed towards the bike.

'We need to get out of here right away!' he said, grabbing a spare helmet and throwing one to Neet.

'What is the matter little cabbage?' asked Alphonsine, 'What has happened?' Suddenly Colette began to bark ferociously. Dr Gore was just metres away, rattling the school gates and screeching like a cockatoo.

'BLEEEEEWIT! BANERJEEEEE!'

'Who is zat?' asked Alphonsine, pulling the sort of face she made when there was too much lemon on her pancake.

'The headmaster!' yelled Frankie scrambling on to the back of the bike. 'Hop in the sidecar Neet, quickly!' Dr Gore was fumbling with his keys and trying to open the gates.

'Yes, yes. Move up, Colette!' instructed Alphonsine, 'Make room for the nice little girl.' Colette sulkily did as she was told and Neet squeezed herself in. 'Let's go!' cried Alphonsine 'You tell me all about it on the way.' Just as the headmaster sprung the catch, Alphonsine's motorbike spluttered into action and lurched away, leaving the headmaster choking in a cloud of fumes.

'Where are you taking us, Alphonsine?' called Frankie through the wind, 'We can't go home. My dad would go barmy.'

'I know,' Alphonsine shouted over her shoulder, 'We need to find a hideout nearby where there are no sticky-pokers. Then you can tell me everything.'

'Oily peas is disgusting filth,' Alphonsine spluttered, 'even for Englishers. Good for ze brain? Pah! What a lot of cowdung! Only thing that is good for the brain is sinking!'

The four of them were sitting in the corner of a small roadside café and, as they tucked into a much-needed pile of pancakes, Frankie and Neet told Alphonsine everything they had seen at Crammar Grammar. They told her about the oily peas, and Snuffles the rat, and the Hole, and the telephone conversation and the Brain-drain machine. Frankie hadn't seen Alphonsine so angry since Mr Blewitt reversed his car over her tulips.

'Sinking?' asked Neet, puzzled.

'Thinking!' Frankie replied.

'Yes, yes, thhhhinking,' Alphonsine corrected herself. 'But Crammar Grammar does not teach thhhinking.'

'We learn lists,' Frankie said, 'then we have tests.'

'It's really difficult,' Neet added, sucking on her orange juice.

'Difficult, maybe,' said Alphonsine, 'but ridiculous also! What is ze point of turning children into parrots?!'

'Shhhh! Alfie!' said Frankie, glancing towards the café owner who was a bit too close for comfort, 'we don't know who's listening!'

'You are right,' nodded Alphonsine, 'Sticky-pokers they is everywhere.'

'But it's important to learn stuff isn't it?' asked Neet.

'Of course!' whispered Alphonsine, 'Very important. But it is what you *do* with it that counts. I give you an example. Let's pretend I am painter. I learn how to mix the colours. I learn how to use the brushes. But if I have no idea what to paint, I still have an empty sheet of paper. Boring yes?' Neet nodded, 'But, if I fill my head with thoughts and dreams and ideas and stories, then I have many things to paint. Zat is the most important bit.' Alphonsine crumpled up her face with displeasure, 'But your little friend, Wesley.

That crawly headmaster suck it all out with his evil hoover! He suck out all his ideas and stick them in a testing-tube. It is terrible. TE-REE-BLE!' Alphonsine was fuming like a frying pan.

'What do you think we should do, Alfie?' said Frankie, 'Dr Gore wants to put all our ideas in test-tubes!'

'He wants to bottle our brains!' said Neet.

'This headmaster is most dangerous,' Alphonsine replied, sucking her coffee thoughtfully. 'But he is not alone. Who, I ask you, was he talking to on the telephone? This person is ze top cheese. Ze big banana!'

'Top banana,' Frankie corrected.

'Yes, yes,' said Alphonsine irritably, 'But cheesy bananas are the most tricky to catch.'

'Whoever Dr Gore is working with,' said Frankie, 'they'll be there on Friday night for the big launch. He's going to show the Brain-drain machine to lots of important people and he wants to use Neet for the demonstration.'

'What?' squawked Neet, 'I didn't hear that bit!'

'You were asleep.' Neet turned pale.

'So, how long do we have, before all the children are turned into zombots?' asked Alphonsine.

'Well today's Thursday,' said Frankie, 'so we have until...' Frankie counted on his fingers, 'tomorrow night!'

'We must make plans,' said Alphonsine, turning to Frankie. 'There is no time to be wasting. We go back tonight!' Alphonsine took a glug of her coffee, 'After I finish my pancakes.'

CHAPTER FIFTEEN
THE TEST TUBE

The friends stayed at the café until night had fallen, then returned to the school on foot so as not to cause any disturbance. Frankie, Neet and Colette slipped through the school gates like water through a weir, but Alphonsine had eaten too many pancakes and had to climb over them instead. She dropped silently to the grass and followed them across the school grounds, through the headmaster's study and down into the secret laboratory.

As the light bulb flickered, Frankie saw that

Wesley was sitting exactly where Dr Gore had left him, as quiet and still as a frightened rabbit.

'Poor little cabbage,' Alphonsine muttered, shrugging off her cardigan and wrapping it around Wesley's shoulders. But Wesley didn't notice. He just kept staring straight ahead of him as if he were about to be hit by a truck. Colette growled angrily at the machine while Alphonsine inspected the tangle of tubes and buttons and levers. 'A proper nasty piece of work,' she muttered, 'Not the sort of thing you leave lying around. Your teacher, he is fruity as a nutcake.'

'Nutty as a fruitcake,' corrected Frankie.

'Same thing,' snapped Alphonsine.

'It works like this,' said Frankie, pointing at parts of the device, 'Dr Gore pulls this lever and this tube here sucks out Wesley's thoughts. Then it takes them all the way along here to...' Frankie stepped back in surprise, 'It's gone!' he cried.

'What's gone?' said Neet.

'Wesley's test tube. It's not here.' Frankie rummaged through the headmaster's poisonous collection of flasks. 'We have to find it,' he exclaimed, 'or Wesley will be stuck like that forever!'

'I'll check the study, Frankie,' called Neet dashing up the stairs. 'It has to be around here somewhere.' Alphonsine studied the machine quietly.

'Now let me thhhhink,' she muttered, 'let me thhhink.' She fished a spanner out of her apron pocket and began to wrench and tug at the machine, umming and ah-ing and muttering things in French. Meanwhile, Frankie and Neet kept on searching high and low. They searched on the shelves and in the drawers while Colette sniffed about under the tables. But Wesley's test tube was nowhere to be found.

'Maybe he has already got rid of it,' said Neet.

'Maybe,' said Frankie, 'but if not, there's only one other place it can be.'

'Where?' said Neet, turning pale.

'With Dr Gore himself. We'll have to get into the headmaster's lodgings.'

'No way!' Neet yelled, 'He'll wake up! He'll catch us! He'll suck our brains out!'

'She is right,' said Alphonsine, 'It is dangerous. You must be veeeeery careful, veeeeery quiet. You must take Colette.' Frankie's belly tightened with nerves. He didn't fancy having his brains sucked out any more than Neet did. But they both knew it was the only way to save Wesley. They pulled up the hoods on their jumpers and crept out of the door.

At the edge of the school stood Dr Gore's magnificent stone house. It was three storeys high with sparkling windows, and the facade was almost entirely covered with a rustling cloak of red and green ivy. As they approached it, Frankie found it hard to imagine that such diabolical schemes could be dreamt up in such a splendid place. The friends crouched behind the low garden wall as they tried to work out a plan. All the windows were dark and empty, making it impossible to tell which one belonged to Dr Gore's bedroom. The last thing they wanted was to wake him. Then they would all have their brains sucked out for sure. They crept up to the front door, but it was locked tight, as were all the ground-floor windows. Frankie stood back and silently scanned the front of the building, looking for a way in.

'There,' said Neet pointing up at the third storey. A single window stood ajar.

'You and Colette keep your eyes open for prefects,' whispered Frankie as he approached the bottom of the wall. 'I think I can climb up the ivy.'

'Alright, Frankie,' whispered Neet, 'but be quick! And stay clear of Dr Gore!' Frankie wedged his foot into the tough branches and began to haul himself up the front of the house. The first few steps were awkward and slippery, but soon he began to find his rhythm. He didn't dare look down, he just kept his hands and feet moving as quickly and as lightly as a spider. When he reached the window, he curled his fingers over the sill and peered cautiously inside.

Frankie strained his eyes to see through the gloom. He could just about make out the shape of a bed and in it the outline of a tall, thin figure ... *Oh, no*, thought Frankie, *It's the headmaster's bedroom!* Dr Gore rolled over suddenly and started sucking noisily on his thumb. Hanging onto the window sill, Frankie scanned the room desperately for a sign of Wesley's test tube, but he couldn't see it anywhere. It was no good; he would have to take a closer look. Quick as a fox, Frankie slipped through the window and padded oh-so-quietly across the carpet, his heart pounding like a hammer. As he walked towards some bookshelves, a dim light beneath Gore's desk caught his eye. It looked like it was coming from the bin. He peeked inside and, to Frankie's great relief, there was the test tube. Its contents glowed a delicate blue, like a puff of bottled sky. *At least the old lizard didn't flush it down the loo*, Frankie thought to himself, reaching towards it. He picked up the tube gingerly and, as he crept slowly back towards the window, he became entranced by the fragile mist inside. Swirling and flickering under his gaze, the mist created shapes and scenes that were as hypnotic as a vision. The outline of a face emerged. It was Wesley and he was laughing as a scraggy dog licked his cheek. *This must be a memory,* thought Frankie, *or maybe a dream*. Then, he saw Wesley as a tiny dancer, jumping like a spark, before a vast, applauding audience. *Definitely a dream!* thought Frankie. The mist shifted again to reveal Wesley's face, but this time he looked pale and worried, frightened even. Yes, he was frightened. He was pressing his hands against the glass walls and staring at Frankie with large, round eyes. No wait. He wasn't staring at him. He was staring at something right behind him.

Frankie lurched forwards as he felt a stiff hand

clutch his shoulder. The test tube flew out of his grasp, struck the ledge and toppled out of the window into the night.

'Wesley!' he gasped. Dr Gore yanked Frankie round to face him and, gripping him by the shoulders, fixed him with a mad, glassy stare. His huge forehead was glistening with sweat and his moustache was twitching like an angry caterpillar. Frankie was certain the headmaster would send him hurtling out of the window after the test tube. But Dr Gore seemed to have other things on his mind.

'Eddie Edison is DEAD, I tell you! DEAD DEAD DEAD!' Frankie couldn't understand what was happening. What was the headmaster talking about?

'I don't know who...' began Frankie, but Gore just carried on raving,

'DEAD! I tell you, DEAD as a DODO!' Then, as

if his batteries had failed, the headmaster released his grip and his eyelids began to droop. Frankie stayed absolutely still and held his breath. Dr Gore's head dropped on to his chest. Then, mumbling something that Frankie couldn't hear, he sloped back to bed, neatly tucked himself under his blanket and started snoring.

Frankie crept backwards towards the window, keeping his eyes fixed on the headmaster in case he had another turn. He had been sleepwalking, that much was clear, thought Frankie as he slipped silently out of the window. But who on earth was Eddie Edison? As Frankie eased himself down the ivy, his heart felt heavier and heavier as if it were slowly filling with sand. He thought about Wesley and the broken test tube. 'Wesley will never be himself again,' he whispered to himself, 'and it's all my fault. I've failed my mission.' As his feet touched the ground, Neet came running up to him.

'You didn't have to chuck it out the window!' she said crossly.

'I'm sorry,' said Frankie hanging his head, 'I didn't mean to.'

'Lucky Colette was there to catch it.' Colette trotted over and sat smartly at Frankie's feet, daintily clasping the test tube between her fine white teeth.

'Good girl, Colette!' cried Frankie flinging his arms around her neck, 'Good girl!'

By the time they got back to the laboratory, Alphonsine had rewired the machine. 'That should do it,' she mumbled, clenching a screwdriver between her teeth, 'I have put it in reverse. Now see what happens.' Alphonsine took the test tube, screwed it in and lowered the helmet onto Wesley's head. Wesley gave a quiet little whimper. 'Don't you worry little rabbit,' said

Alphonsine, patting him on the knee, 'You will be better soon.' She wiped her brow on her sleeve and grabbed the lever. 'Stand back!' she cried and pulled hard. The machine sprang into action, kicking up such a racket that Frankie was afraid it would wake the whole school. Wesley gritted his teeth and dug his nails into the palms of his hands as the machine began to suck Gore's dark gas out of one ear, while the contents of the test tube trickled steadily into the other. As it emptied, Frankie could see Wesley slowly turning back into his normal self. He blinked his eyes and creased up his forehead like he was concentrating on a really difficult question. Then his face lit up like a bulb.

'Did I get it right?' he asked excitedly, 'Did I win?'

CHAPTER SIXTEEN
MONSIEUR L'AMBASSADEUR

'Quickly, all of you!' cried Alphonsine, rushing them back to her motorcycle, 'We must get out of here before your headmaster smells a fish. We are going to pay a visit to an old friend of mine. He will help us.'

Poor Wesley felt quite queasy as Alphonsine's motorcycle dodged through the streets of London like a crazy bluebottle.

'What's happening? Where am I? Ooooooooh, my head feels terrible,' he wailed.

'Don't worry Wes!' Neet shouted over the

traffic, 'You'll be okay now!' Wesley felt so weird he didn't even mind being called Wes.

'Thank you, Neet,' he whimpered.

After what felt like an age, Alphonsine's motorbike pulled up outside a grand old building with tall, glowing windows.

'We will stay here tonight,' Alphonsine said.

'Wow!' said Frankie. 'Does your friend live here?'

'But, of course,' said Alphonsine, pulling off her helmet, 'Where do you expect the French Ambassador to live? Up a tree?'

'She knows the French Ambassador?' whispered Neet. Frankie shrugged his shoulders in amazement and followed Alphonsine up the fine marble steps. An official-looking Frenchman with a nose like a shark-fin opened the door narrowly.

'What do you want?' he snapped.

'Tell *Monsieur l'Ambassadeur...*' Alphonsine leaned forward and whispered something through the crack. Straight away, the official flung the door open and bowed so low Frankie thought he'd turn a somersault.

'An honour Madame, it is an honour! Ze Ambassador is in his pyjamas but he will be so happy to see you.'

'*Ma chère*, Alphonsine!' A grand old fellow in a velvet dressing gown and nightcap flounced down the marble hallway and kissed Alphonsine's hand. '*Quelle joie! Quel honneur!*' Alphonsine tapped him on the shoulder.

'*Monsieur l'Ambassadeur*,' she said, gesturing towards her companions, 'My friends do not speak French,' The Ambassador gasped and clutched his chest as if he had been stabbed.

'But I am shocked!' he cried, 'Why ever not?'

Neet and Frankie shuffled their feet awkwardly, but Wesley, who had been pretty quiet till now, suddenly piped up.

'*Bonsoir,*' he ventured, '*Bonsoir Monsieur l'Ambassadeur.*' The Ambassador was thrilled to bits.

'Ha ha! *Bonsoir! Bonsoir!*' cried the Ambassador shaking their hands, 'You see, Alphonsine. They *do* speak French. I think they have earned their *chocolat chaud, non?*' Wesley smiled. He was feeling better already.

The Ambassador led them all into a cosy sitting room with enormous plush sofas and a chandelier that winked in the light of a smouldering hearth. Then, with a snap of his fingers, an impeccable waiter appeared balancing a platter of hot chocolate and biscuits on his white-gloved fingertips.

'You may not know it,' said the Ambassador

as he dunked a jammy dodger into his cup, 'but Alphonsine is not only my oldest and bestest friend, she is also a true heroine.'

'*Oh la la*! Stop it *Monsieur l'Ambassadeur*!' chuckled Alphonsine, 'You embarrass me!'

'During ze war,' he continued, 'Alphonsine and I were in the same resistance unit. She was the bravest, most clever *saboteuse* of them all. One time, she blow up a whole truckload of weapons. BANG! BANG! BANG!' shouted the Ambassador stabbing the air with his fingers, 'Like fireworks.'

'Happy days!' said Alphonsine, shaking her head, 'But now, *Monsieur l'Ambassadeur*, we have another battle to fight.'

'Oh, yes? he said, licking a blob of jam off his thumb, 'Tell me all.' Frankie and Neet told him everything. The Ambassador shook his head and said '*Oh la la*!' over and over again while Wesley sat there in stunned silence as he listened to what Dr Gore had done to him.

'It's dreadful,' he said. 'My parents just want me to have a good education. If they knew what Crammar Grammar was really like, they'd go spare.'

'Outrageous!' the Ambassador exclaimed once they had finished their story, 'Outrrrrrrrrrrageous! My dear Alphonsine, I am at your service. I must make a telephone call,' he said, standing up to leave the room, 'but you must tell me straight away if there is anything you need.'

'Thank you, my friend,' said Alphonsine. She turned to face Frankie, Neet and Wesley, her eyes glittering like boot buttons. 'We must make plans,' she said. 'There is little time.' But Frankie wasn't paying attention.

'Wake up, Frankie,' said Neet, nudging his

shoulder.

'Sorry!' He jumped to attention, 'I was just thinking about something Gore said when I was in his room.'

'You spoke to him!' said Neet in amazement.

'Not really. He was sleepwalking. He was having a nightmare. He just grabbed me and started shouting.'

'What did he say my little cabbage?' asked Alphonsine, 'Tell us.'

'He said, "Eddie Edison is dead," and then he kept repeating it, "dead, dead, dead." He was all sweaty and shaky. He almost looked scared.'

'Who's Eddie Edison?' asked Wesley.

'I don't know,' said Frankie, 'Maybe he was a pupil here. One that didn't get rescued.' Wesley shuddered.

'Or maybe it's the top banana,' said Neet hopefully. 'You know, the big cheese. Maybe he snuffed it?'

'Perhaps,' said Frankie, 'What do you think, Alfie?'

But Alphonsine did not answer. She looked pale and shaken as if a ghost had just drifted through the room. Finally, in a slow, trembling voice, she whispered, 'Eddie Edison was my very darling husband.'

CHAPTER SEVENTEEN
EDDIE EDISON AND LUCAS REGO

'Your husband knew Dr Gore?' asked Frankie, astonished.

'No!' said Alphonsine, 'At least, I do not think so. My husband went missing a very long time ago.' Alphonsine dabbed the corner of her eyes with a tissue. 'And now he is dead. My poor Eddie.' Neet put her arm around Alphonsine's shoulders.

'I'm so sorry, Alfie,' said Frankie. 'That's awful.' Alphonsine blew her nose loudly.

'Yes, awful,' she said. 'But Eddie is missing so long. I already know that he is gone forever. It was not like him to disappear just like zat. So very strange.' Alphonsine shook her head in bewilderment.

'Maybe if you told us what happened,' said Neet kindly, 'we could make some sense of it all.' Alphonsine sighed and clasped her hot chocolate between her trembling hands.

'After ze war,' she began, 'Eddie and me, we moved to England and Eddie opened a pharmacy. He was a chemist, and a very good chemist also. When somebody was poorly, he had always some special medicine that would make them right as a raindrop. He would go into his garden and pick his herbs. Then he mash them and boil them and mix them with honey. He had a special medicine for every bug and beastie on ze planet. Except for one.'

'What was that?' asked Wesley.

'Ach!' replied Alphonsine, slapping her

forehead in frustration. 'What you call it when you is sneezing and wheezing and thinking your nose will explode?'

'A cold?' ventured Frankie.

'Yes, yes, a cold. The common cold.'

'Nobody has ever found a cure for the common cold,' said Wesley, 'it's impossible.'

'Aha!' Alphonsine raised her finger, 'Eddie never say impossible. He was working so hard to find a cure. All the time, the house is full of germs. Then, one day I is icing my cupcakes when I hear a shout from Eddie's laboratory. Well, the icing goes all over the place and I am most cross. I say: "Eddie! What is the matter? You spoil my cupcakes!" and he looks at me, happy as a hamster, and says, "Darling Alphonsine, I have done it!" Well straight away he is in all the newspapers and there is photographers tramping over my daffodils. Everyone was saying it was the greatest scientific discovery since gravity. He was even nominated for the Bowbell prize.'

'The most important science prize in the world,' said Neet, swapping glances with Frankie.

'Yes, I was so proud,' said Alphonsine. 'So he is working hard to make his cure tip-top. Then one day he goes out to buy the final ingredient... and never comes back. Ever.' Alphonsine heaved a deep and terrible sigh.

'That's awful,' said Frankie, 'What happened to him?'

'I do not know,' said Alphonsine, shaking her head, 'I look for him up and down, left and right, but he vanish. And because he never wrote down the formula for his cure, it is still hankies and hot water for everyone. Such a pity.'

'And who won the prize?' asked Frankie.

'The prize was won by some other cleverbody,' Alphonsine continued, 'but, not long after the prize-giving, the winner was disqualified.'

'Disqualified?' said Neet.

'Zat is what I said,' said Alphonsine, 'It turns out the winner was a cheat, a liar, as crooked as my nose. He fibbed his results so he'd look more clever than he actually was, but he was soon found out.'

'Did they put him in prison?' asked Frankie.

'No. He run away with all the prize money and is never seen again.'

'What was his name?' Frankie asked cautiously. Alphonsine hesitated a moment, then replied, 'His name was Lucas Rego.'

'Lucas Rego?!' cried Frankie, jumping to his feet.

'But of course,' said Alphonsine, looking puzzled.

'We saw his prize in Dr Gore's study,' gabbled Frankie, his mind racing. 'There's a certificate on the wall and it's got Lucas Rego's name on it.'

'But it is impossible,' gasped Alphonsine.

'It's true,' said Neet, 'We saw it.'

'But how could the headmaster know him?' asked Wesley, folding his arms.

'I dunno,' said Neet, 'Maybe they knew each other at school. Or maybe they're related.' Frankie frowned in concentration – he had a hunch, but he wasn't sure he was right. He grabbed a pen and started to scribble on the back of a napkin.

'Perhaps that's it, Neet,' said Frankie, 'perhaps they're very closely related.'

'What are you doing little cabbage?' asked Alphonsine as Frankie jotted down a jumble of letters.

'C – A – L –' he muttered under his breath.

'What are you writing Frankie?' asked Neet. Frankie looked up at his friend and smiled.

'I've got it. I know how they're connected.'

'Really?' asked Wesley, creasing his brow. 'How?'

'What's Dr Gore's first name?' Frankie asked.

'Calus,' Wesley answered quickly.

'Right,' said Frankie, 'and if you rearrange the letters of Lucas Rego, what do you get?' Neet thought for a second.

'Calus Gore!' she cried, 'It's him! It's him!'

'Yes!' said Frankie, 'Dr Gore is Lucas Rego. They are the same person. That's why he knows Alphonsine's husband.' Alphonsine gasped and pressed her hands together.

'Yes. It must be so,' she murmured.

'It all makes sense,' said Frankie. 'Dr Gore, or Lucas Rego, knew that your husband, Eddie, had almost perfected his formula. And he knew that if Eddie found the cure for the common cold then he would win the Bowbell prize for sure.'

'The prize that Dr Gore wanted more than

anything in the world,' added Neet.

'Exactly,' said Frankie, pacing up and down in front of the fireplace like a detective unravelling a great mystery. 'There was no way he was going to let anybody take that away from him.' Neet clenched her fists in fury.

'So he must have done away with Eddie then claimed the prize and all the prize money for himself!' she exclaimed. 'That's terrible!'

'That's right,' continued Frankie, 'But, because he's a cheat and he'd never made a Big Discovery of his own, he got caught out and had to go into hiding. That's when he changed his name to Dr Calus Gore.'

'He's a murderer,' murmured Wesley, beginning to shake, 'My teacher is a murderer!'

'Not just that,' said Neet, 'he's not a proper scientist either. He just invents any old rubbish, then tests it out on us.' Frankie noticed that

Alphonsine was sitting very quietly, staring into her chocolate.

'We'll stop him, Alfie,' said Frankie. Alphonsine scratched her glass eye in thought, and lifted her head.

'Yes,' she said, 'We will stop him once and for always.'

By midnight, the Ambassador's sitting room had been transformed into a council of war. The friends worked late into the night devising plots and plans to stop Dr Gore. Neet wanted to tie the headmaster to a rocket and send him into outer space, while Wesley thought it would be more sensible to tell the newspapers. But Frankie wasn't convinced.

'The trouble is,' said Frankie, 'Nobody is on our side. Dr Gore has invented a machine that turns children like us into prize-winners – our

parents will love it, the teachers will love it. Nobody *wants* to stop him.'

'They're not all as mad as he is,' said Wesley.

'But they trust him,' said Frankie. 'They see all his certificates on the wall and they think he knows what he's doing. They think he's doing what's best for us.' Frankie wasn't wrong. In fact, the problem was simple. If one child was turned into a prize-winning super-computer then how were the others supposed to keep up? Parents would simply be clamouring for their children to be given the treatment and before long every school in Britain would be equipped with a shiny new Brain-drainer. The thought made Frankie's blood run cold. He shuddered and shoved his hands deep into his blazer pockets. As he did so, his fingers touched something small and round and a little bit manky. The Telitol tablet! Frankie examined the tiny green capsule, and a germ of an idea began to take root. He wrinkled his nose in concentration and turned the tablet between his fingers. Then, suddenly, as if a bulb had come on in his head, Frankie knew exactly what they had to do.

By the time they had thought through Frankie's plan from every possible angle, the sun was peeking over the horizon and the Ambassador had appeared with a basket of hot pastries.

'There's one last thing,' said Frankie, munching on a croissant, 'How are we going to get near the launch event? Dr Gore will recognise me straight away'.

'Easy-peasy,' said the Ambassador. 'In my Resistance days, I was master of disguises, was I not dear Alphonsine.'

'Yes, most masterful,' she nodded.

'I fix you up in no time!' said the Ambassador, 'Nobody will suspect a thing.'

'Then we must go back,' said Alphonsine, 'No more time for chatterboxing.'

'She's right,' said Frankie, 'We need to get Wesley back to the lab where Dr Gore left him, or he'll smell a rat.'

Wesley was chewing on his croissant like a nervous squirrel. 'Does that mean I have to get back into that machine?' he stammered.

'Afraid so, Wes,' said Neet, 'or Gore will know something's wrong.' Wesley gulped down hard.

'I wish I'd never volunteered,' he whimpered, 'I just wanted to be head boy, that's all. I just wanted Mum and Dad to be proud of me.'

'They will be, Wes,' said Neet, giving the small boy a hug, 'You're going to be a hero!' Colette yelped excitedly. She smelt something in the air. They all did. It was the smell of adventure.

CHAPTER EIGHTEEN
THE BIG CHEESE

Frankie and Alphonsine crouched in the shadows and watched silently as Dr Gore's guests began to arrive.

'Does my disguise look alright?' asked Frankie, tugging at his false moustache and beard. 'Do you think they'll let us in?' Alphonsine looked Frankie up and down. Frankie looked like a small boy in a silly beard, but it was too late to do much about it.

'Just keep ze hat down over your face,' said Alphonsine, tipping the brim. 'And try not to trip over your shoelaces.'

'Okay,' sighed Frankie nervously, pressing his moustache into place. He peeked out from behind a wheelie-bin, trying to avoid the glare of headlights. The guests were rolling in thick and fast. There were lots of extremely serious looking people with mobile phones glued to their heads, and groups of learned types speaking cleverly and pushing their glasses up their noses. There were teachers, scientists, journalists, government ministers, eggheads of every variety and even the odd popstar. But everyone was there for one thing and one thing only. As a clever-looking lady remarked, as she wandered dangerously close to their hiding place, they were there to witness the dawn of the Brain-Age.

'Let's go!' said Alphonsine, tugging at Frankie's elbow.

'No, wait,' said Frankie, 'Look. They've all got tickets'. Frankie was right. The guests were brandishing fancy-looking cards at Mrs Piggot who was standing at the door with a face like a bulldog. Frankie and Alphonsine watched in dismay as a ticketless reporter tried to slip past, only to be lobbed into the flowerbed by Mrs Piggot's huge right arm.

'Ouf!' puffed Alphonsine. 'Always complications! But we cannot wait. Follow me.' To Frankie's surprise, Alphonsine made a beeline for a popstar who was so busy blowing kisses to photographers that she didn't notice a sly old woman picking her pocket.

Alphonsine and Frankie sat quietly at the back of the assembly hall as the guests jostled their way to their seats and squabbled for places near the front. On the stage was an impressive-looking lectern for the headmaster to speak from and, next to that, a small table with a glass and a jug of water. But, at the back of the stage, concealed by a swathe of red velvet, was the thing that everybody had come to see: Dr Gore's masterpiece. There was a kerfuffle at the door as Mrs Piggot told the popstar that she didn't give a monkey-nut who she was – no ticket, no show. Then the lights dimmed dramatically and everybody hushed.

Dr Gore strode onto stage, grinning like a pantomime genie. He was wearing a glamorous fur-trimmed robe and his moustache looked as if it had been fluffed up with a hairdryer.

'Thank you, thank you!' he smirked, as he took his place behind the lectern, 'You really are most kind.' The headmaster flashed his eyes around the room and Frankie sank down low in his seat. 'Ladies and gentlemen,' Dr Gore began, 'I have served this school for many years and have worked tirelessly to provide the very best education for our children.' The audience murmured sympathetically while Frankie spluttered in disbelief. 'It is a competitive world,' the headmaster continued, 'and parents today know that they must give their children every advantage they can over other people's children. It's only natural.' There was a rumble of disquiet in the audience, but the headmaster steamed on, 'I have devoted many years of my life to polishing even the dullest minds but, as many of you know, my first calling was as a man of science.' Dr Gore liked the sound of that, so he said it again, 'A man of science! What you shall witness here today, ladies and gentlemen, is something of my own design, something quite revolutionary, something that will transform even the simplest Simon into a clever Trevor. After all...' Dr Gore put his hand to his heart in a gesture of concern, 'we only want what's best for the children.' The audience nodded enthusiastically and there was a brief splutter of claps. 'But research of this kind would not have been possible without the generosity of people who, like myself, are truly passionate about learning.'

'Now he is talking about the big cheese,' Alphonsine whispered to Frankie, 'The fellow on the phone. The one who is paying for all this nonsense.' Frankie nodded and sat up in his seat to get a better look.

'So, before I proceed,' said Dr Gore, smiling like a conger eel, 'I would like to take this opportunity to thank my most noble, most admirable, most generous sponsors, Mr and Mrs Blewitt!'

Frankie's eyes stretched wide in horror. *No!* He couldn't have heard right. But, sure enough, his parents stepped out of the front row to a thunderous burst of applause. Alphonsine shook her head and cursed in French as Mr Blewitt

strode on to the stage. Seizing Dr Gore's hand in a manly handshake Mr Blewitt pumped his arm up and down so hard Frankie thought it might pop out of its socket.

'Good man, Calus!' bellowed Mr Blewitt, pounding the headmaster on the back. Taking the stand, he addressed the audience while Mrs Blewitt smiled so ferociously Frankie thought her face would ping off.

'I know a good idea when I see one,' Mr Blewitt began, swelling up like a blowfish, 'and I'm the kind of guy who puts his money where his mouth is...' Frankie couldn't bear to listen. So that's why Dr Gore couldn't say no to Mr Wallet. His dad was paying for all the headmaster's experiments and, in return, Dr Gore took Frankie off his parents' hands. It was what his dad would call a win-win situation.

'This is what I'd call a win-win situation,' bellowed Mr Blewitt. 'The parents are happy, the teachers are happy and the kid's a genius. Everyone's a winner. And, as I like to say, if you can't win it – it's not worth it.' Mr Blewitt flexed his shoulder muscles for effect and returned to his seat to waves of applause.

Frankie felt a dreadful mixture of fear and anger boiling in his belly. 'I don't know if I can do it, Alfie,' he stammered, beginning to panic, 'I didn't know they would be here. It's not part of the plan. It's not part of the plan at all!' Alphonsine squeezed his knee and looked him in the eye.

'Adventures cannot always be planned,' she said, 'Is normal. Have no fear little cabbage.'

'But my dad will squash me! He'll never let me come home!'

'Do you *want* to go home?' asked Alphonsine, looking at him with serious grey eyes.

'No, but...'

'Well, then,' said Alphonsine, 'There is nothing to fear. Remember little cabbage, "F" is for Frankie, "F" is for Fantastic!' Frankie knew she was right. He breathed deeply, trying to untwist the knot that was tightening in his stomach.

Dr Gore took centre stage. 'It's almost time,' he rasped, flashing his triangular teeth, 'But first...,' he paused for effect, '... here's one I prepared earlier.' Gore clicked his fingers and

Wesley, acting as zombie-like as possible, marched on to the stage, staring robotically. The audience shifted in their seats to get a better look.

'Wesley isn't meant to be here,' Frankie whispered anxiously, 'I thought he would use Neet.'

'And here,' the headmaster clicked his fingers once more, 'is the raw material.' Neet peeked round the curtain then shuffled awkwardly on to the stage.

Phew, Frankie heaved a sigh of relief. Dr Gore turned to the audience. 'Now, ask them a question,' he instructed, 'Any question. As difficult as you like.' Frankie glanced at Wesley and saw him swallow hard. If he couldn't answer the question, then Dr Gore would know something was wrong.

A teacherly looking gentleman near the aisle put up his hand.

'What did the Owl and the Pussycat go to sea

in?' he asked gently. *A pea-green boat!* thought Frankie, *that's a good one.* But the headmaster was not impressed.

'My dear sir,' he scoffed, 'Who cares? A serious question please.' A very earnest-looking lady in half-moon glasses raised a finger.

'What...' she began, 'is the square root of one hundred and forty four?'

'Anita,' the headmaster sneered, 'perhaps you'd like to answer the lady's question?' Neet looked at the ceiling, then looked at her feet.

'I don't know, Sir,' she mumbled. Dr Gore rolled his eyes in amusement and some of the audience chuckled.

'Now, Wesley,' Dr Gore said, crossing the stage, 'Do *you* have the answer?' Wesley hesitated, wrinkling his forehead in concentration.

'Come on, Wes!' Frankie whispered under his breath, 'Please get this one right!'

'Quickly now!' spat the headmaster through a clenched smile. Wesley bit his lip and counted on his fingers behind his back. Dr Gore's eyes started to glow a filthy yellow as the audience raised unimpressed eyebrows. Then, all of a sudden, Wesley's face lifted, 'Twelve!' he announced. The audience exploded into cheers and Dr Gore mopped his enormous forehead.

'Lucky he is a brainbox,' nodded Alphonsine seriously. 'Not even I know the answer, and I know many things.'

'Now,' crowed Dr Gore, 'I will reveal the ingenious device that transforms children like that,' he jabbed a finger at Neet, 'into children like this!' he pointed at Wesley. The crowd fell silent in anticipation and craned their necks to get a better view.

Dr Gore had been sweating so heavily that he was extremely thirsty. So before moving on to the most important part of his demonstration he picked up the jug and poured himself a large glass of water. Frankie crossed his fingers and hoped that Neet had managed to carry out her part of the plan. As the headmaster drained the glass, Frankie saw Neet giving him a slow wink. It was time for Frankie to make his move.

CHAPTER NINETEEN
THE TRUTH

With a dramatic flourish, Dr Gore pulled away the velvet drapes to reveal the Brain-drain machine. It had been carefully buffed and polished and was as bright and shiny as one of Mr Blewitt's cars.

'Behold the Mind-enhancer!' bellowed Dr Gore like a circus ringmaster. The audience gasped and started scribbling in their notebooks.

'Mind-enhancer, pffff!' Frankie muttered, 'It's a Brain-drainer.' Dr Gore grabbed Neet by the elbow and marched her towards the machine.

This was Frankie's moment.

He scrambled on to his chair and put up his hand.

'Dr Gore!' he shouted, 'I have a question!' The headmaster froze and spun round, searching the audience for the speaker. 'I have a question, Dr Gore,' Frankie repeated. Everybody turned around to see who had dared interrupt. Frankie stood up tall and hoped that nobody would recognise him. But his false beard came unstuck and swung loose from his ear. The audience gasped. *A child!* What was a child doing amongst such distinguished company? Frankie tried to slap the beard back on but it was too late.

'Frankie Blewitt!' squawked the headmaster. Frankie glanced towards his parents. They were looking the other way, pretending Frankie had nothing to do with them, but Frankie could see

his father's ears steaming with rage. 'Now, now,' hissed Dr Gore through gritted teeth, trying to sound headmasterly, 'Children aren't allowed in here, unless they are part of the experiment. Mrs Piggot! Would you please take this child back to his dormitory?'

'One question, Sir!' Frankie insisted.

'No!' Dr Gore snapped, 'absolutely no questions. Mrs Piggot!' The audience began to mutter in dissatisfaction. Mrs Piggott pulled Frankie from his chair and dragged him towards the door. But before she had the chance to throw him into a flowerbed, a clear voice echoed round the hall.

'Wait.' A woman who had been seated alone at the side of the hall, rose to her feet. She was tall and smart with sharp, intelligent eyes. Dr Gore's very important guests gasped in surprise. There was somebody present who was even more important than themselves. The

Prime Minister.

Dr Gore began to quake with joy. The Prime Minister had come to witness the unveiling of his Big Discovery! It really was more than he'd hoped for! Perhaps she would make him a Lord, or an Earl or a Duke or...

'Dr Gore,' said the Prime Minister.

'Yes, Prime Minister?' quivered the headmaster.

'This is a school, isn't it?'

'Yes, Prime Minister, the very finest...' The Prime Minister didn't let him finish.

'And schools are for asking questions, am I right?' Dr Gore didn't dare say she was wrong.

'Yesssss... Prime Minister,' he grimaced.

'Well, then, let him ask his question.' Dr Gore had no choice. Mrs Piggot reluctantly dropped Frankie on the floor and the Prime Minister motioned for him to begin. Frankie spoke as loudly and clearly as he could, so that the whole hall could hear.

'My question, Dr Gore, is…' Frankie looked the headmaster straight in the eyes, '…who is Lucas Rego?' The audience began to babble in confusion and some of the sciencey types raised their eyebrows in astonishment. They hadn't forgotten the story of the rogue scientist who had hijacked the Bowbell prize, all those years ago. But none looked more astonished than Dr Gore. The headmaster cackled nervously as if it were the stupidest thing he had ever heard.

'Lucas Rego? What are you talking about Blewitt? I've never heard of a…' Then, as if he were about to be plunged underwater, Dr Gore drew a deep sharp breath. Frankie glanced at the glass of water on the table. The Telitol tablet that Neet had slipped into the headmaster's jug was beginning to work! Dr Gore's eyes bulged like ping-pong balls and he clamped his lips together to try to stop himself speaking. But the tablet was much too powerful to resist. After all, Dr Gore had improved the formula himself. 'I...' he spluttered, '...I am Lucas Rego!'

The audience could hardly believe their ears. Frankie walked up the aisle towards the stage and towards the headmaster who was clasping his throat as if he were about to choke himself.

'And who...' Frankie pressed on, 'is Eddie Edison?' Dr Gore's tongue shot out of his mouth and began to twist horribly as he tried to prevent himself from speaking. But it was no use.

'Eddie Edison,' spat Dr Gore, 'discovered the cure for the common cold. The greatest discovery... since gravity.'

'So how come *you* won the Bowbell prize instead of him?' Frankie continued.

'Yes!' shouted a member of the audience, 'How come you won?' Dr Gore fought back the words, but the formula was too powerful.

'I ch...ch...ch... I CHEATED! Then I ran away to ch... to ch... to CHILE! And I ch...ch... CHANGED MY NAME!' The audience gasped in outrage as the headmaster spat and writhed and twisted himself in knots. But Dr Gore couldn't help himself. 'I came back...' he continued, '...and bought the school with the pr...with the pr... with the PRIZE MONEY!'

'Why did you buy a school?' asked Frankie.

'For my EXPERIMENTS of course! Children make quite excellent g...g...g... GUINEA PIGS!'

The audience was jumping and hissing like a vat of exploding popcorn. 'Cheat!' they shouted, 'Fraud! To think we trusted you with our children! You're as mad as a mole!' Sensing trouble, Snuffles the rat dived out of the headmaster's pocket and took refuge amongst the tubes and wires of the Brain-drainer.

The headmaster was green with rage, but Frankie hadn't finished. He had one last question. He stepped up to the front of the stage. 'Did you kill Eddie Edison?' he asked. Alphonsine twisted her hands together and waited for the reply. Spluttering and hissing like a malfunctioning robot, Dr Gore produced a cackle that made Frankie's blood freeze.

'Kill him?' the headmaster screeched hysterically, 'That really would have been a waste! No. I did something much worse! Much, much worse!' The audience sprang to their feet, booing and hissing and throwing their notepads.

'What do you mean?' cried Frankie, 'What did you do to him?' but the audience were shouting so loudly Dr Gore couldn't hear. He staggered backwards under a hail of pencils and, as he did so, he caught his foot on a cable. The headmaster teetered for a second, flailing his arms, then he toppled backwards, straight into his own contraption. As soon as he touched the seat, the helmet dropped down and locked itself on to his head. The headmaster was still laughing and hooting hysterically as the Brain-drain machine roared into action, shaking and lurching and pumping out clouds of dark, purple smoke.

The audience stared in shocked silence. Something was wrong. Frankie stepped forward to look at the machine and saw that Snuffles, in a bungled attempt to escape, had become completely jammed in one of the pipes. The Brain-drainer spat a swarm of sparks into the first row and shuddered violently as the pressure built.

'Stand back!' Frankie shouted to Neet and

Wesley. Then, in a huge purple flash, the machine went off like dynamite.

KERPOW!

CHAPTER TWENTY
THE SCANDAL

The guests screamed and charged towards the exit, knocking Frankie sideways as they pushed past. Frankie scrambled under a bench and watched herds of feet stampede past him. His head was pounding and the sound of the explosion rang in his ears. Noxious, purple fumes had filled the hall and Frankie pressed his sleeve to his mouth to stop himself from choking.

As the last guest bolted out of the door, Frankie squinted through the smoke. His vision was blurry but he couldn't miss the pair of highly polished shoes that were planted just inches away from his nose. Frankie looked slowly up the perfectly pressed trouser legs to see a huge angry face glowering down at him.

'FRAAAAAAAAANKIIIIIE!!' growled Mr Blewitt, yanking Frankie out from under the bench and hoisting him off the floor by one skinny ankle. Mr Blewitt was so choked with rage he could hardly speak.

'Let go! Dad! Let me go!' yelled Frankie. But Mr Blewitt just clenched his fist tighter.

'Put him down,' said a stern voice. Mr Blewitt spun around to see who had dared give him an order. It was the Prime Minister, and she was flanked by five sturdy police officers. Mr Blewitt dropped Frankie like a hot crumpet.

'What's going on?' squealed Mrs Blewitt, staggering towards them, her face covered in soot.

'Mr Magnus Maxwell Maximilian Blewitt,'

said one of the police officers, 'Mrs Camilla Camelia Cordelia Blewitt. You have the right to remain silent.'

'What?' puffed Mr Blewitt, 'What are you talking about, man?'

'Yes! What *are* you talking about,' squawked Mrs Blewitt, turning rather pale.

'You are both under arrest for funding criminal activity,' the Prime Minister explained. 'It is clear to me that you were hoping to profit from Dr Gore's ghastly invention. You can both expect a good few years in the clink. Isn't that right, officers?'

'That's right, Madam,' replied a policeman gruffly.

'This is outrageous!' stormed Mr Blewitt, 'This is a SCANDAL! I want a lawyer! I want ten lawyers! People like us don't go to jail. Are you mad?' While the policemen wrestled Mr Blewitt into a pair of handcuffs, Mrs Blewitt, sensing an opportunity to escape, hitched up her skirt and made a dash for the emergency exit. But, before she could pick up any speed, a burly policewoman tackled her to the ground.

'But it's not fair!' she bawled as she was marched out of the door, 'I only wanted the best for my little Frankiepops! Tell them Frankie! Tell them you want to come home with your mummy and daddy!'

'You'd better do what your mother says young man!' bellowed Mr Blewitt, 'You'd better stop this mucking about right now!'

But Frankie didn't want to go home. He didn't want to go back to being pushed around and shouted at and locked in his room. He didn't want to be his mum's prize-poodle or his dad's trophy-son. He just wanted to be Frankie.

'Sorry, Mum,' he said quietly. 'Sorry, Dad. I

don't want to come home. Not if things are going to be the same as before.'

"Course not!' said Mr Blewitt, spotting an opportunity to bargain. 'You can have that new computer game, and a new robot and you can stay up as late as you like! I'll even let you read a comic, what do you say?'

'That's quite enough wriggling!' said the Prime Minister, losing patience, 'You'll have plenty of chances to keep those promises. But first both of you need to spend some time thinking about what a brilliant little boy you have, IN JAIL. Now stop whingeing and get in the police car!'

As the police sirens screamed into the distance, Frankie felt quite alone and a little afraid. But he also felt as if a huge weight had been lifted off his shoulders. For the first time in his whole nine years, he wasn't scared of getting things wrong, or messing up, or not being good enough. He didn't know where he would go or what he would do next but he felt sure that, whatever happened, it would be his own adventure.

'You and your friends have been very brave. Real heroes.' The Prime Minister was looking down at him like a concerned rescue dog. Frankie smiled proudly.

'Frankie?' Neet peered out from behind a curtain, 'Is it all over?'

'Neet!' called Frankie, jumping to his feet, 'Where's Wesley?'

'Here!' Wesley shouted, crawling out from under the stage, 'We did it! We did it! It was fantastic Frankie!'

'This is Neet and this is Wesley,' said Frankie.

'I know,' said the Prime Minister. 'My good friend, the French Ambassador, called me late last night and he told me all about your adventures. I could hardly believe his story, so I came down here to see for myself. You have done a great job, all of you.' The three friends beamed with pride.

Suddenly, a ferocious squeaking was heard coming from the wreckage of the Brain-drain machine.

'Snuffles!' Frankie exclaimed, running towards the smoking wreck. Sure enough, Snuffles the rat was still lodged in the tube and squealing for all he was worth. But something about him had changed. Frankie looked more closely. Snuffles's eyes were no longer a pale pink. They were an acid yellow.

'Come and look at this!' called Frankie. The others gathered around him. As they listened to Snuffles's enraged squeaking, they began to make out some tiny, angry words.

'Bleeeeeeeewit!' he squealed, 'Banerjeeeeeeee!'

'It's Dr Gore!' cried Frankie, 'He's in Snuffles's body! Look!' Neet, Wesley and Frankie clutched their sides in laughter as Dr Gore ranted and raved and pulled at his whiskers in fury.

'Where's Alphonsine?' cried Frankie, 'She has to see this!' But Alphonsine was gone.

CHAPTER TWENTY-ONE
LE PAPILLON

'Alfie! Alfie!' shouted Frankie, racing out of the building. Alphonsine was sitting alone on a low stone wall. She gave Frankie a big smile, but her eyelids were red and puffy.

'Well done, little cabbage,' she said, slapping him on the leg, 'Well done.'

'I'm sorry, Alfie,' said Frankie, sitting down next to her. 'We still don't know what happened to Eddie do we?'

'No,' she replied, ruffling Colette's ears, 'Maybe we never know.' Frankie and Alphonsine sat together quietly for a while. Alphonsine stared at the night sky overhead, but Frankie couldn't stop thinking about Eddie Edison and his mysterious disappearance. There was so much that just didn't add up.

'When I was in Dr Gore's room, he kept saying that Eddie was dead,' said Frankie, turning the facts over and over in his mind, 'But it turns out he didn't kill him.'

'Perhaps someone else kill him,' replied Alphonsine, scratching her nose.

'Maybe,' said Frankie, 'but I get the feeling the headmaster just wanted people to *think* Eddie was dead.' Frankie creased his brow in concentration.

'*Le Papillon?*' A voice derailed Frankie's train of thought. He glanced over his shoulder. The Prime Minister was striding towards Alphonsine, with Neet and Wesley trotting behind. 'You must be *Le Papillon*. Am I right?' Alphonsine looked utterly startled.

'Of course,' she said, blushing and shaking the Prime Minister's hand, 'But it is years since I hear zat name!'

'Our friend the Ambassador has told me so much about you. It is an honour to finally meet you.'

'What's going on, Alfie?' asked Frankie, struggling to keeping up.

'*Le Papillon*,' said Alphonsine, 'It was my code-name during ze war.' Wesley stuck up his hand like he was still in class.

'It means butterfly in French,' he explained, smiling up at the Prime Minister.

'Why butterfly?' asked Frankie.

'Ach, you ask so many questions!' replied Alphonsine, 'Butterfly: a creature with eyes zat cannot see.' She winked at him with her false eye, 'that is why.' Frankie's mind began to race. He felt like he was holding the last piece of a giant jigsaw puzzle. If he could just work out where to put it.

'I'm afraid I must get back to London,' said the Prime Minister, signalling to her driver. 'I've got an early start tomorrow. But I expect to see you all at Number Ten soon. I'd like to thank you properly for your wonderful detective work.' The Prime Minister shook everybody's hand, 'You all deserve a gold medal.'

'A gold medal,' Frankie murmured to himself as the Prime Minister's car rolled out of sight, 'Gold.' Then, as if by magic, everything slotted into place. 'Alfie,' ventured Frankie cautiously, 'I think I know what happened to your husband.'

'Don't be silly, Frankie,' replied Alphonsine, shaking her head, 'I know you is wanting to help. But it is impossible.'

'No really, Alfie,' Frankie insisted, feeling

more and more certain that he had struck on the truth, 'There's somebody who can show us. Come with me.'

Goldie was at home stirring some milk into a cup of tea and reading his favourite book for the billionth time. By the time he got to the end, he had already forgotten the beginning, so he just read it over and over again. It was one of the few good things about having a memory like a Swiss cheese. As he flicked through the pages, Frankie and his friends gathered quietly outside.

'What is this nonsense Frankie?' muttered Alphonsine through chattering teeth, 'My bones are chilly. It is time to go.'

'Just a minute, Alfie,' said Frankie, knocking on the shed door. 'There's someone you have to meet.' Frankie could hear Goldie's slippers shuffling across the floorboards. 'He doesn't remember much,' Frankie explained, 'So don't be surprised if...' Goldie opened the door and peered outside.

'Well hello young man,' he smiled, spotting Frankie, 'What can I do for you?' Alphonsine gasped and pressed her hands to her chest. Then she fainted dead away.

Goldie looked down at the elderly Frenchwoman, blinking in confusion.

'Oh, dear! Dear oh dear!' he stammered, running to fetch a cold sponge to dab on her face.

'Madam?' he said, crouching down and shaking her gently, 'Are you alright?' Alphonsine opened her eyes slowly.

'Eddie!' she whispered, 'Is that you?' Goldie put on his spectacles and steadied himself on the doorframe. A memory, or a shred of a memory, had slowly begun to float to the surface. Wrinkling his brow, he searched Alphonsine's face as if he

were trying to see to the bottom of a deep, murky lake. 'Eddie, Eddie, It *is* you! I was thinking you was dead, Eddie!' A large tear rolled down Alphonsine's cheek as she crawled to her knees and clasped the porter's hands. He stared back at her like a startled bird caught in the paws of a giant cat. Then he shook his head and looked down, worried and confused.

'It is Alphonsine, Eddie,' she murmured sadly, 'Alphonsine.' But it was no use. Goldie could not remember. Then, all of a sudden, he squeezed Alphonsine's hands tightly. He had seen something. Frankie looked and saw a large blue mark on Alphonsine's forearm. He had noticed it before and always thought it was a nasty bruise. But this time he saw something else. Etched on to Alphonsine's wrist was a faded tattoo of a butterfly. Goldie's cloudy eyes suddenly began to clear.

'The loveliest butterfly in the world,' he stammered, looking up at her as the light of a memory began to flicker, 'Alphonsine?' Alphonsine grinned from ear to ear and flung her arms round her husband's neck. Goldie, or rather Eddie Edison, lifted Alphonsine to her feet and happily ushered everybody into his shed. There were so many memories that had failed him completely, but this one never had. 'Come in! Come in! Come out of the cold!' Goldie sang, throwing down some cushions for his guests to sit on, 'I'll put the kettle on!'

As Goldie and Alphonsine fussed over the stove like a pair of happy budgies, Neet and Wesley huddled around Frankie.

'How did you work it out, Frankie?' they asked, 'How could you know?'

'Do you remember when we were in the lab,

Neet?' said Frankie, 'and there was a shelf stacked with Dr Gore's potions?' Frankie opened Goldie's fridge, took out a carton of milk and held it under Neet's nose.

'Yuk! Euurgh!' Neet pushed the carton away. It stank of mouldy cheese. 'How could I forget that!'

'Right,' said Frankie, turning to Eddie. 'Eddie,' he asked, 'Can you tell me where you get your groceries from?'

'What's that got to do with anything?' asked Wesley, folding his arms.

Eddie scratched his head with a teaspoon. 'Well, um, now let me think. I'm not allowed to go out myself. I'd never find my way back you see. So Dr Gore brings me my groceries every morning. Bread, cheese, tea and milk. It's all I need. I'm not fussy.'

'That's what I thought,' Frankie replied, 'This isn't ordinary milk Eddie. This is the milk we found in Gore's laboratory. This is Milk of Amnesia.'

'What's amnesia?' asked Neet, wrinkling up her nose.

'It's when you forget everything,' explained Wesley. 'So what you're saying Frankie, is that Eddie has been stirring Milk of Amnesia into his tea for years. Dr Gore has made him forget his past, forget who he is... everything.'

'That's right,' said Frankie. 'What could be better for Dr Gore, than to have his old rival working for him, taking his orders and living in a shed. The headmaster said so himself. Killing him would have been a waste.' Alphonsine ruffled Frankie's hair, 'So clever Frankie!' she smiled, 'I could not have done better myself!'

'Well then,' blinked Eddie, 'I assume we'll be drinking our tea without milk. How very French.'

'The effects should wear off now you've

stopped drinking it,' said Frankie, 'So hopefully you'll remember everything soon.'

'Well that would be a treat,' said Eddie, smiling at Alphonsine, 'But for now, I remember enough.'

CHAPTER TWENTY-TWO
SNUFFLES

The next morning, the pupils of Crammar Grammar were surprised to find that they had slept in until ten o'clock. Usually Dr Gore's voice rattled over the tannoy at six o'clock sharp to shake them out of their beds and into their lessons. But that morning, the speakers were silent. The children were even more surprised when the headmaster failed to turn up for assembly. Something very strange was going on, that much was clear. The assembly hall looked like a junkyard, and there was a huge black hole at the centre of the stage. Shrugging their shoulders, the pupils shuffled off to their classrooms where they expected to find yet another test waiting for them. But there was no test, and no teachers. You see, in order to avoid getting mixed up in Dr Gore's mess, every single teacher had done a runner in the night.

So, the children had the school to themselves. As there was nothing going on in the classrooms, they wandered slowly out into the fields. The air was crisp and sunny and there was a thin crust of snow on the ground. The students blinked their eyes as if emerging from a daze. Then one of the first years scraped up some snow in her hands, packed it into a ball and lobbed it in the air. Then somebody else did the same... then another... then another. Within seconds the school had exploded into an almighty snow fight. The children built snow fortresses, caught snowflakes, sucked icicles and squealed as their friends shoved snowballs down their backs. For the first time in years, it was playtime at Crammar Grammar.

Meanwhile, Frankie and his team were eating an almighty fry-up at the Prime Minister's house in Downing Street. The Prime Minister wasn't a very good cook, but she had made it herself as a special thank you. As her guests got stuck in, she asked Wesley, Neet and Frankie about the sort of school they would really like to go to. Wesley rabbited on for hours while the Prime Minister diligently scribbled notes, but Frankie was too preoccupied to listen. He turned to Alphonsine and Eddie.

'What do we do now?' he said, pushing his scrambled egg around his plate. 'We haven't got a home, I haven't got a school and Mum and Dad are in prison.'

'I don't know, little cabbage,' sighed

Alphonsine, 'we think of something. We always think of something.' Frankie smiled, but at that moment he was completely out of ideas.

'I have an idea,' interrupted the Prime Minister. She turned to Eddie, 'It is clear to me, that Calus Gore cheated you out of your prize money. If he hadn't kidnapped you and made you forget who you were, you would certainly have won the prize. So I suggest you all move into that lovely stone house at Crammar Grammar. By rights it belongs to you.' Eddie looked embarrassed, 'Do you mean the headmaster's lodgings?' he asked.

'Of course. It's a bit big for Dr Gore now, wouldn't you say?'

'Well,' smiled Eddie, 'I do have the keys.'

'A home, Eddie!' gasped Alphonsine, squeezing her husband's hand. 'How wonderful!' Alphonsine put her arm around Frankie's shoulders, 'You will live with us little cabbage. It will be tip-top!'

'In the meantime,' continued the Prime Minister, 'I will get my best ministers to sort out that school. New teachers, new lessons, no more tests. It will be the model for every school in the country, just you wait and see!'

When the pupils came back from their Christmas holidays, Crammar Grammar was a new place altogether. The statue of Dr Gore had been taken away, the bars had been removed from the windows and the barren playing fields had been marked out with goalposts. In fact, Neet turned out to be a very talented footballer. So talented that even her mum came to see her play – though Neet wished she wouldn't shout so much from the sidelines. Wesley, meanwhile, stopped spending so much time revising and discovered that he was as great a dancer in real life as he was in his dreams. He landed a part in the school musical and skipped and twirled down the corridors on the way to his lessons. And what brilliant lessons they were! The grey classroom walls fluttered with colourful drawings, maps and diagrams, and the classes were packed with fascinating facts, stories and ideas. Frankie even discovered, to his great surprise, that he loved reading. Now that he no longer had his dad looming over him with the *Encyclopaedia Brittanica*, he could read whatever books he fancied. So he read about famous adventurers and the far-off lands they had travelled to. Then he read about brilliant scientific discoveries and the French Resistance and lots of other things besides. And when the bell rang for playtime, he went outside and he played and played and played.

'Hey, Alfie,' called Frankie, as he came home

from school one day, 'Guess what?'

'What, my little cabbage?' replied Alphonsine, polishing her motorbike.

'We've got a class pet!'

On a shelf, in the science lab, a white rat scuttled round and round in its cage. The rat had twitchy whiskers, an angry little squeak and yellow bulging eyes. Only Frankie and his friends knew who he really was. Everyone else called him Snuffles.